DAHLIAS AND DEATH

PORT DANBY COZY MYSTERY #6

LONDON LOVETT

WILD FOX PRESS

CHAPTER 1

*K*ingston swooped down from the blue summer sky and landed on the shop roof. His long, black beak swung around like the arrow on a weather vane as he scanned the area for other crows. It seemed he was out of luck this morning. My phone rang as I parked my bike along the side of the building.

My mom always managed to catch me just as I was leaving from or arriving at work, even today when she and Dad were just hours away from their visit to Port Danby. "Hey, Mom, I just got to work. Are you guys getting packed?"

"Getting packed? We're already at the airport."

"Why? Your flight isn't for five hours." I swung my backpack, my traveling bike purse, as I liked to call it, off my shoulders and rummaged through the front pocket for my keys.

"Well, we didn't know how much time security would take. There's the whole taking your shoes off thing and making sure we're not carrying tiny bottles of liquid."

"If it's taking you five hours to pull off and put on your shoes, then we need to start looking for one of those special homes for you two."

Kingston cawed and dropped down to the sidewalk. He'd been hanging around humans more than birds and had somehow concluded it was more appropriate to walk into a building than fly.

"Oh shush, smarty pants," Mom's voice chirruped through the phone. It was surrounded by the usual airport clamor. "We like to make sure we're early in case they move the flight up."

Kingston's talons click-clacked on the shop floor as he marched toward his perch in the window.

"Mom, it doesn't work that direction. They don't suddenly say 'hey, you know what? The skies are clear and the pilot got here early so hop on the plane we're leaving'. They delay flights. They don't move them up." I flipped on the lights. The interior of my colorful, fragrant and, if I did say so myself, chicly designed flower shop came into view. "Hey, Mom, I've got to get the work day started. I'll see you guys this evening." I hoped that was my perfect segue to hanging up but then, it was Mom on the other side.

"Wait, Lacey, I called for a reason other than your sweet, lovable sarcasm," she said, her tone dripping with the stuff. "Now if Dad and I die in a huge ball of flames somewhere over the ocean—"

"You're not flying from another continent. No possibility of that unless the pilot decides to take the scenic route. Flying is very safe, Mom. You'll be fine." I walked into my tiny back office to put away my backpack and start my computer.

"Easy for you to say, you're not flying with the man who forgot to pack his gas pills."

My dad's annoyed tone seeped through from somewhere nearby. "That's right, Peggy, tell the whole airport about my gas pills."

I turned my face away and smothered a laugh.

"Mom, I've got to start my day. I'll see you soon. Looking forward. Have a safe flight." I tried for another hang up but without success.

"Yes, well if *that* isn't the case. Just remember the important papers are inside the metal cabinet in the hallway closet."

"Yes, got it. Love you. Bye." I hung up before she could recite all the old family recipes that might otherwise go up with her in the ball of flames. It seemed I was destined for an exhausting week.

The bell rang as I logged onto the computer.

"I'm here, boss." Ryder poked his head into the office. My absolutely perfect assistant had recently decided on a more mature haircut. His usual tuft of long bangs no longer hung over his forehead. The new look highlighted his blue eyes and playful smile. "Thought I'd design a few red, white and blue bouquets for the holiday. What do you think?"

I flashed him a very nineties thumbs up. "When do I ever say no to your ideas, especially wonderful ones? Those dark blue larkspur stalks leftover from the wedding party would be perfect."

"Just what I was thinking. Great minds think alike."

"Please," I said, "if only I had half the mind and memory as you. It took me ten minutes to remember where I placed my cup of coffee this morning. Finally found it on top of Kingston's cage. By then it was cold."

Ryder stepped further into the office. "You're just rattled because Mom and Pop Pinkerton are coming for a visit. Can't wait to meet them."

I stood from the desk chair. "I am looking forward to showing them around Port Danby." I followed him back out to the front of the shop.

"And Pink's Flowers," he added enthusiastically.

"Actually, if there was one place I could skip on the tour, it would be the shop."

Ryder spun back around with a look of surprise. I realized now

3

that he had nice, expressive eyebrows. The long bangs always hid them. "Why is that?"

I sighed and looked around. "I love the way my shop looks, but my mom will find many things wrong with it. Mark my words."

"I'll bet you a free piece of pie at the diner that she'll walk inside and be awestruck."

I put out my hand. "Deal. Think I'll try Franki's new peanut butter chocolate delight."

"We'll see." Ryder walked behind the work island and grabbed Kingston's treat can. He pulled out a few snacks, sending the bird into his usual song and dance routine. "Do you have a date for the Port Danby Fourth of July Celebration yet?" he asked as he handed the crow treats and then quickly and wisely pulled his fingers away from Kingston's beak.

I took yesterday's orders out from under the counter and sat on the stool to go through them. "I didn't realize a date was required. Which probably answers your question." I perused the orders, making sure I had everything I needed. "How about you?" I asked without looking up from my task.

His silence grabbed my attention. My face popped back up. Ryder avoided looking my direction.

"Uh oh," I said. "Do you mean to tell me the most handsome, eligible guy in town is dateless for the big festivities?" I regretted my taunt the second I finished it. After more than six months working with Ryder, I knew exactly what his brooding expression meant. "Just ask Lola. The worst that can happen is she says no." The strange, tentative on again, off again relationship between Ryder and Lola sort of mirrored the one between Detective Briggs and me. So I had no right to give advice so confidently, but I could see he was hurting. And, unfortunately, my best friend Lola Button's middle name was fickle. I knew she liked Ryder, but if he showed too much interest she tended to scurry off like a frightened deer.

Ryder looked relieved when the bell rang. Elsie hurried in holding a tray of something that immediately overwhelmed my supersonic nose. My hyperosmia, or extreme sense of smell, allowed me to catch and decipher even the slightest scents. Normally, I worked to keep my olfactory cells under control so as not to end every day with a pounding headache. But whenever Elsie walked in with one of her mouthwatering treats, it was hard to hold back.

"I definitely smell blueberries and strawberries."

She placed the dish on the counter. The dessert was covered with a carpet of bright blue, heavily glazed berries, plump and round with deliciousness.

I took another whiff. "Cream cheese. Graham crackers."

"This is my good friend Nicole's Blueberry Delight. Only I added strawberries for the holiday to make it Red, White and Blueberry Delight. I made it for your parents."

"Then you've already won my dad's heart. My mom's too, but she'll be less generous with the praise." For some unexplained reason, I worried that Elsie and Mom would not get along. I hoped it was just my intuition being thrown out of whack by the busy holiday week.

The Blueberry Delight dish was too big for my little office refrigerator. "Can you keep it in your bakery fridge for now? Ryder and I have our mini refrigerator pretty cluttered with tea, water and soda."

"Sure thing. Didn't you say you had a garden club meeting today?" Elsie's smile was more of a rub than amusement. She found it humorous that I'd somehow gotten talked into joining the Port Danby Garden Club. Today was my first meeting since joining. I was actually looking forward to it. Elsie seemed to think I'd regret my decision, but she tended to be somewhat cynical. Why was I thinking Elsie and Mom wouldn't hit it off? They were peas in a pod.

"First meeting right after lunch. It should be fun." I said confidently to assure her I was still thinking positively about my new membership.

Elsie's nose crinkle was one part skepticism, one part humor. "I'm sure it will be lovely. As long as Molly and Carla don't get into their usual spat about who grows the most fragrant roses. Of course, at the moment those two are going to be more at war about the Port Danby Pie Contest than their garden accomplishments."

"Aren't you entering the contest?" I asked.

Elsie followed me as I headed to the potting side of the shop for vases. "No. About five years ago, the powers that be, not sure who exactly, decided since I was a professional baker I could no longer enter my pie. My buttermilk pie won every year, so most people didn't even bother to enter."

"I guess that makes sense." I plucked a clear, cylinder shaped vase and an opaque white flower bud vase from the shelf.

Elsie made a scoffing sound behind me. "Only now, Molly Brookhauser wins every year with her cinnamon apple pie. Not sure how that's any different. Anyhow, I've got to get back to the shop. I've got brownies in the oven. I'm decorating them with fudge frosting and red, white and blue fondant stars. I'll bring you one later when I bring the dessert back."

"And you know now that you told me, I'll be waiting for that brownie all day. Thanks, Elsie."

She stopped at the door and called back to me. "Are you making a basket for the picnic auction?"

"Hadn't given it much thought." I returned with my vases to the work island. "I probably won't bother."

"Too bad. I'll bet that handsome detective is looking forward to bidding on it."

I rolled my eyes and shooed her out. My earlier worry was silly. Elsie and Mom would hit it off just fine.

CHAPTER 2

The midday sun was hotter than I anticipated as I rode along Culpepper Road. Normally, an ocean breeze wafted in after lunch to relieve the summer heat, but today the air was so still it was almost eerie. Even the local birds had taken to the higher tree branches to wait for the anticipated refreshing breeze.

Hot or not, I always loved a bike ride along Culpepper Road. The road was on the far west edge of town. It was lined with small, quaint farms. Jenny Ripley, president and today's hostess for the garden club meeting lived on Maplewood Road in a charming yellow Victorian surrounded by a scenic acre of land. She had recently retired from her librarian job in the town of Mayfield. She now kept busy with her garden and embroidery.

I turned off Culpepper and onto Maplewood. Several cars were already parked out front of Jenny's house. The club was small so they were anxious to have me join. I figured it could only help my standing in the community to be part of some of the local groups.

Who knew, maybe someday Mayor Price would even learn to trust me and no longer consider me an outsider.

I could see Jenny's bright yellow apron in the backyard as I pedaled the bike up to the porch. Jenny's house was the quintessential nineteenth century farmhouse with its wraparound porch and gabled roof. A white picket fence surrounded a nice patch of grass and flowers in the front yard. The fluttering purple, pink and white petals of sweet peas snaked along the porch railing, filling the air with their candy scent. The property itself stretched deep behind the house. An old stone wall running between her lot and the neighbor's was in the process of being torn down. Oddly enough, the posts being set for the new fence were at least three feet to the left, making Jenny's plot of land even larger.

Jenny looked up from the table where she was placing plaid green linen placemats. Her bright yellow apron was embroidered with orange tabby cats. No doubt one of her own creations.

Carla Stapleton came out of the back door carrying a tray of lemonade. Carla was an interesting sort. I'd only met her twice. She was tall for a woman, maybe five foot ten or eleven and she had nice sturdy shoulders to go with it. I hadn't met her husband Vernon yet but Elsie had warned me not to let my mouth drop too far. Apparently Vernon was a good six inches shorter than his wife and a great deal smaller than her in every way. I guessed Carla to be in her forties. She had no children, unless you counted her twelve pet chinchillas. Which apparently she did because I'd already seen numerous pictures of her furry babies engaged in any number of activities that a chinchilla might engage in. (Which wasn't saying much.) Of course, who was I to judge when just this morning I sternly reminded my crow to pick up all of the cereal he dropped on the carpet as if telling my kid to pick up his room.

"Lacey," Jenny practically sang my name as she spotted me in the yard. "So glad you made it. Carla and I were just getting lunch ready. The rest of the members should be arriving any minute." Jenny hurried back into the house.

"Can I help?" I called on her way past.

"No, just enjoy some refreshment." The screen door snapped shut as she disappeared inside.

Carla handed me a glass of lemonade. "Here, you look like you could use this. Did you ride all the way on your bicycle?"

"Yes. I was hoping for an ocean breeze during the journey but it's late today."

Carla stopped to fan herself. "You're right. That's why I'm feeling so darn hot." Her smile dropped and her square jaw jutted forward as the garden gate opened and shut behind me.

I turned back to see who had arrived. Molly Brookhauser walked in wearing a sparkly red, white and blue baseball cap. It was a dazzling conglomeration of sequins, rhinestones and silver star studs. Molly beamed as she noticed how our eyes were instantly drawn to it. There was no way to avoid the over-whelming sparkle. Molly was a forty-something divorcee with twins in college. She had short brown hair that she liked to tuck behind her ears, even while it was under a hat. Jenny had mentioned that Molly lived just down the street from her.

Molly pointed up at it, though that was hardly necessary. "How do you like it? I bought it at the Mod Frock. Kate told me it's one of a kind. I'm wearing it to the fireworks show."

"It looks heavy," Carla said dryly. Elsie had predicted right. The tension between the pair was pretty instant as Molly turned her lip up in response.

The screen door creaked open. "Oh my gosh," Jenny chirped from the back porch steps. Her focus was on the hat, only I wasn't getting a 'what a fantastic and glorious hat' vibe from her as she crossed the lawn. "Where did you get that?" she asked with irritation.

Molly's brows crunched together in confusion. "I was just

9

telling the girls that I bought it from Kate Yardley. She said it was 'one of a kind'," both Jenny and Molly said in unison.

Jenny turned around with a harrumph and marched back into the house, only to emerge seconds later with another of Kate's one of a kind patriotic hats.

Carla shrugged. "Probably your first mistake was believing Kate. She's a shrewd saleswoman. She once talked me into a pair of short boots that were at least a size too small. She told me they made my feet look petite."

I nodded. "Yeah, Kate is a master at the backhanded compliment."

"I wore them for about ten minutes to a party that Vernon and I went to over in Mayfield. I had to walk around barefoot all night. And she wouldn't take them back because she said they were too stretched out."

That comment earned a laugh from Molly. And the laugh earned a heavy browed scowl from Carla. It seemed there was more than a touch of animosity between them.

I stepped up to plate as the new member, showing I had plenty to offer to the group. "Since there is no rule that says you can't wear matching hats, I say you both show up sparkling with patrio-tism. Besides, it might make Kate squirm to see both of you in the hats. Maybe she won't be so deceptive next time." (Yes, my offer of help included a tiny bit of revenge on Kate but not undeserved.)

Jenny and Molly seemed to mull my compromising solution for all of two seconds before both simultaneously saying no.

"That wouldn't do at all," Molly said. "After all, Jenny is twenty years older than me. How would it look if we showed up making the same fashion statement?"

Jenny looked properly miffed but she washed it quickly away. She appeared to be the negotiator and peacekeeper of the bunch. "How about if we both agree not to wear the hats to the celebra-tion? There is still plenty of time to wear it this July."

Molly nodded reluctantly. "I suppose that makes sense."

Two more members arrived, including Virginia Kent, an elderly woman whose neighbor and main pumpkin growing contest competitor Beverly died in a terrible tragedy last October. She walked in with a man, who looked to be about her age, late seventies. They were holding hands which was the cutest darn thing I'd seen all day.

"Hello, everyone," Virginia called cheerily. I hadn't seen her much since her neighbor's murder, but she was looking much more spry. That might have been due to the charming man next to her with a head of white hair and an ingratiating smile. "Hope you don't mind. Oscar wanted to join us today."

Carla leaned over to fill me in on a few details but because she was several inches taller than the rest of us, it was awkwardly obvious. "They met on a senior's matchmaker site. He's a retired podiatrist. Virginia's been acting like a blushing schoolgirl ever since."

"How wonderful." I stepped forward to greet them. "How do you do? I'm Lacey Pinkerton. I own Pink's Flowers."

Virginia recognized me instantly. "The pretty girl with the powerful nose," she said. "How is that handsome devil—" She tapped her chin with a brightly pink polished nail. "What's his name?"

"Detective Briggs is fine." I shook Oscar's hand too.

"If we all take a seat," Jenny said, "we can have some refreshments before we start the meeting."

Carla made a point of pulling out the chair farthest from Molly. I followed quickly behind Jenny. "I'll help you carry out the food."

"Thank you, Lacey." Jenny's house was immaculate with labels on every kitchen drawer and each coffee cup hung neatly on a hook. I instantly wished I'd done a better job straightening up my house for my parents' visit.

I glanced at the half demolished wall through the side kitchen window while waiting for Jenny to pull sandwich trays from her refrigerator.

"It looks like you're getting a new fence."

Jenny turned with a grunt of exasperation. "That wall has given me more gray hairs than my thirty years of work combined." Her hazel eyes glittered with amusement at her own comment. Jenny seemed to be the most likable of the club so far. "This property belonged to my late husband's mother. He inherited it about ten years into our marriage. Percy Troy, my neighbor," she stated the name with no small amount of consternation, "inherited his property from his Aunt Henrietta. Apparently, Aunt Henrietta was the one who decided to build that old stone wall to divide the properties. Only she did it without having the land surveyed for proper dividing lines. Well, the wall has started crumbling. Every time it rains, another stone falls out. I hired a surveyor to find the exact lines for the properties so we could build a new fence. It turned out Henrietta had the wall built a good three feet on my side." Jenny handed me a tray of pretty tea sandwiches and reached into her fridge for a second platter with fruit and cheeses. She closed the refrigerator door with her hip. "When I mentioned to Percy that I'd go halves with him on a new fence but that the new fence would move three feet his direction, he threw a fit. The man is as cheap as Scrooge, himself. Not only did he not want to put up a new fence, he most assuredly did not want to give up any property."

Jenny managed to open the screen door with her elbow and waved me through, continuing her story as we carried the food outside.

"We ended up in a court battle. He lost, of course. And the judge told him that since his aunt made the mistake in the first place, he would have to pay for the new fence on his own."

"Oh my, I'll bet that made him even more sour."

"You could say that," she said. "It's rather sad. Anyhow, being the miserly man that he is, he decided to demolish and rebuild the new fence all on his own. And he is no spring rooster."

"He sounds rather stubborn," I said as I placed the sandwiches down on the table.

"Stubborn and cheap," Jenny said. "Now everyone dig in so we can get down to club business."

CHAPTER 3

*J*enny's egg salad and cucumber on pumpernickel were just what I needed to reenergize myself after the long, hot bike ride. Thankfully, the much anticipated after-noon breeze kicked up as well. It seemed everyone was in a cheerier mood once the fresh air danced around Jenny's yard.

Oscar, it turned out, was quite hard of hearing, Virginia patiently repeated everything talked about at the table. Molly was beyond agitated at having to listen to everything retold, verbatim and at an extra loud volume. Her lips were in a thin, grumpy line by the time Jenny started the meeting. They grew thinner when Jenny asked Carla to read the last meeting's minutes.

Carla's eye rounded. "Me? Why of course. Let me just grab my glasses. You know I can't see a thing without them."

Molly grunted with aggravation next to me but Carla didn't hear. "She can't see a thing *with* them either," Molly muttered.

Carla returned, excited about her task. Along with the glasses, she carried a tube of sun block. She quickly applied some to her nose and cheeks. "Anyone else? The sun is straight above at this time."

Jenny and I took her up on the offer. As I spread some on my nose, Molly snorted. She held out her forearms. "I never need that greasy stuff. I only tan."

Oscar, who couldn't seem to hear one word at lunch, somehow heard her comment and jumped right into doctor mode. "It doesn't matter if you only tan, everyone can get skin cancer."

That medical advice, true as it was, only made Molly's posture slump more. She was not having a good club meeting. I wondered if that was usual or if she was just in a particularly bad mood.

Molly had not exaggerated about Carla's eyesight. The reading of the minutes, which was no more than half a page and contained little information, took a good fifteen minutes mostly because very patient Jenny had to help Carla read every other word. Carla complained the font was far smaller than average but it seemed to be just fine.

Carla finished the minutes. Molly wasted no time starting the meeting with a suggestion, although she said it more as a demand. She stood from her chair, cleared her throat and tucked her hair behind her ears. The sequined hat sat on the table. Halfway through the drawn out reading of the minutes, the hat seemed to get too heavy. I noticed her discretely trying to crack her neck a few times to relieve the burden of the weight on her head. Something told me Kate's one of a kind hats were not going to be the next big summer fad in Port Danby.

"I propose that we add a rule to our garden club constitution." Molly stood up straight, projecting her voice as though addressing congress.

"We have a constitution?" Virginia asked.

Molly waved off the perfectly reasonable question. "I think, since we represent the local gardening community, we should be role models for the rest of the town. We should never plant flowers that are already blooming. We should start our gardens from scratch like true experts, from seeds, tubes and bulbs. Just recently, I discovered Carla transplanting the dahlias in her garden straight from the nursery pots. It's a terribly amateurish move and more than a little dishonest."

Despite the sun block, Carla's face turned a beet red. It was a mix of anger and embarrassment. Unusual for me, I was stunned speechless by the baseless attack. Jenny jumped to Carla's aid before she melted into a shame filled puddle beneath the table.

"Molly, it just so happens that I went to the plant nursery with Carla. She was looking for dahlia tubers but they were sold out. She was very set on having dahlias in her garden and was terribly disappointed." Jenny touched her chest. "I told her she should buy the pots of dahlias and replant them in her garden. And frankly, you're being very harsh, Molly."

Carla still looked shaken, but some of the red was cooling from her cheeks. Molly, feeling properly chastised by the club president, sat down without another word. Carla was silent too.

"You know, I think the sun is just a little too hot for us today," Virginia said. "Oscar and I are going to leave early."

Jenny got up to walk them out. I was left at the table with Carla and Molly. The temperature was hot but the atmosphere at the table was cold as ice.

"I must confess, I replant flowers from the nursery into my garden for instant color," I said.

My comment earned a weak smile from Carla, but Molly pretended to be interested in the metal star studs on her hat. I breathed a sigh of relief when Jenny returned to the table. Elsie was going to want to hear every detail of the club meeting so she could say 'told you so'. And that she did. She told me so, indeed.

Jenny picked up a pen and opened her notepad. "We need ideas for the garden club booth. We need to set it up tomorrow. Then we'll need to make sure someone is running the booth during the festivities. It would be great if we could sell something for a fundraiser."

"How about potted dahlias?" Molly said snidely with a sideways glare at Carla.

"How about potted herbs?" I piped up quickly. "I'd be happy to donate them. I've got basil, oregano, thyme and rosemary at the shop."

Carla's smile returned. "What a wonderful idea. But would you be able to get the pots planted in time? The celebration is the day after tomorrow."

"No problem. I'll get started on them right away."

Jenny clapped lightly. "I love that idea. All in favor?" Even Molly had to begrudgingly say *aye*. Especially when she didn't seem to have anything else constructive to add to the meeting after her short rant about the dahlias.

Jenny drew a quick chart on her paper. "I'm going to set the booth up tomorrow. You can bring the herbs whenever you have them ready. And since you're doing all that work, Carla, Molly and I will take turns running the booth."

I picked up my lemonade. "That works." The shop had been quiet since the start of summer, so I had plenty of time to get the herbs planted. As we firmed up details about the booth, a swarm of busy body flies began darting around the leftovers on the table.

Jenny waved her hand to clear them away, but flies were never scared off by a hand wave.

"It seems the flies are on to us. We should probably take this food back into the house," I suggested.

"Good idea." Jenny reached for the sandwich tray, and I picked up the second platter.

Molly snapped her hat down low on her head. "Well, if there's nothing else to discuss, I promised to help Rachel Holder make salt water taffy for the city council booth. They are raising money to refurbish the Hawksworth Museum."

I forced back a smile at the term museum. An old gardener's shed stocked with a few mismatched and uninteresting artifacts was hardly a museum, but it was the town's claim to fame, along with the century old murder mystery.

"Refurbished? How?" I asked. Molly had, after all, tripped onto one of my favorite subjects. I held my breath hoping for something groundbreaking and exciting.

"I think there is talk of painting the outside of the gardener's shed," Molly said.

My shoulders dropped in disappointment but then I wasn't sure what I was expecting.

Molly lifted her lemonade and drained the glass. She set it down on the table but got a proper librarian-like look of disapproval from Jenny.

"Since I made the lunch, it would be nice if you at least helped by bringing in the glasses," Jenny said.

Molly plucked up the glasses with a huff, reminding me of a teenage version of myself being asked to clear the table.

Carla seemed anxious to put space between her and Molly so she hurried ahead carrying in the leftover napkins and placemats.

The four of us gathered in Jenny's immaculate kitchen, admiring her organized pantry, complete with brightly colored labels on every basket and container. Even Molly dropped her grump face and took a picture so she could try something like it in her own kitchen. Carla snapped a photo as well. And while I couldn't see myself organizing my kitchen any time soon, I felt obligated to show the same enthusiasm.

Carla looked at the photos she'd snapped. "If you don't mind, Jenny, I'm going to post these on my food and garden hobby blog. I've just earned my three hundredth follower," she said with a beaming smile.

Thankfully I was the only person to catch Molly's eye roll. I'd had enough contention for one club meeting. It was now glaringly obvious that Molly didn't like Carla. And while she didn't show her aversion as boldly, I could only assume that Carla also didn't care for Molly.

Jenny closed the pantry doors. "Ooh, I have one more little part of the house tour to show you. My dad left me a rather impressive collection of World War II memorabilia. It'll just take a second, if you guys have a moment to spare."

I needed to get back to the shop but Jenny seemed so excited to show us the collection, I didn't have the heart to say no. Even Molly politely followed Jenny down the narrow hallway to a bedroom at the back of the house. The interior of the house was spotless but outdated. The bedroom we entered had an antique wrought iron daybed that was adorned with dozens of embroidered pillows, at least two for every holiday.

Jenny laughed lightly and picked up a pillow with a bright orange Jack-O'-Lantern embroidered on black fabric and another with a gray bunny holding a colorful basket of intricately hand-stitched Easter Eggs. "I store these in here until the corresponding holiday comes around. Right now, I've got two flag pillows on the sofa in the front room." Jenny practically skipped over to the closet on the side wall. She threw open the doors to expose shelves filled with war artifacts. Before she could start her 'tour' the front door-bell rang.

"I wonder who that could be?" Jenny turned to us before leaving the room. "Go ahead and browse. I'll be right back."

The shelves were filled with faded uniform patches, several intricately carved knives, a canteen and mess kit and many black and white photos. It was a nice little collection, but I badly needed to get back to the shop. And I was standing with my two garden club counterparts who'd fallen awkwardly silent during Jenny's absence. Fortunately, she returned quickly with another pair of footsteps plodding down the hallway behind her.

A fifty something man wearing thick glasses and a blue cap

over what appeared to be a mostly bald head walked in after Jenny. His face was pink, and there was a line of sweat around the collar of his shirt as if he'd been working out in the sun.

"Everyone, this is my neighbor, Percy Troy." Jenny's tone was slightly off, as if she was forcing politeness. Apparently, this was the cheap, stubborn neighbor with the wall problem. "He dropped by to ask a question, and I mentioned I had the war memorabilia collection out. So he decided to join us."

Percy nodded politely to all of us and stepped farther into the room to see the collection.

Jenny briefly talked about the medals and the pictures, before pulling forward a box made of polished walnut. The brass plaque on the front said *World War II Commemorative Colt 1911.* "This was my father's prized possession." Jenny opened the box to reveal a well-preserved handgun with an intricately embossed silver-plated grip. Even the barrel was ornate. Eight shiny bullets had their own separate compartments in the dark blue velvet interior of the display box.

Percy and Molly seemed most interested in the collection, but Carla's attention was pulled to the embroidered pillows.

I gave my due attention and complimented the items before making my exit. "Jenny, if you don't mind, I've got to get back to the shop and get those herbs planted."

"Of course."

Supreme hostess that she was, Jenny walked me out to the front porch and waved good-bye as I climbed onto my bicycle and pedaled down the driveway.

CHAPTER 4

*R*yder had taken a late lunch. I'd finished potting basil and rosemary in tiny plastic pots and was leaning into the sink washing my hands when the shop door opened. "I'll be right with you," I called.

Something cold and wet pressed against the back of my knee. I tossed a handful of suds into the air with a stunned gasp. I spun around to find Detective Briggs' dog, Bear, sitting politely behind me, pretending the cold nose had nothing to do with him. Briggs shrugged apologetically at me. He wasn't wearing his usual suit and tie. It was just too hot. His white dress shirt looked exceptionally nice against his tanned skin. His dark hair had grown just a touch longer. It curled up nicely on his white collar.

I patted Bear on his big, soft head. I'd never been as confused about anything as I was about my relationship with Detective James Briggs. I was solid about a few things. I liked him a lot and not just in a 'hey let's have a cup of coffee' way. I loved working murder cases with him. And I would certainly not say no if he moved toward a kiss. *Certainly not.* But just when I thought things were heading that direction and we grew even more comfortable with each other, he got distracted by work or I got busy at the shop. But it wasn't just the usual logistical barriers and life happens kind of stuff that got into the way. There was something else. And whatever it was, it came totally from his side. He withdrew whenever it seemed we were moving forward. I'd finally convinced myself that he just didn't feel the same way I felt. It felt like a cold slap in the face knowing Briggs just wasn't that into me, but I had no intention of risking a perfectly good friendship over a broken heart.

Briggs walked over to say hello to Kingston. My bird gave him a cursory glance before returning his shiny black eyes to the two sparrows twittering outside on the window ledge.

"What time do your parents get in?" he asked. We hadn't spoken in a week. Briggs had been working on a case in the neighboring town. They were all small towns but sometimes it seemed he had to stretch himself thin to cover the three neighboring coastal cities as well as Port Danby. I only wished I could use that as the excuse for him not having enough time to see me socially.

"Well, as long as the plane didn't leave early—"

"Early?" he asked with those dark eyes that always seemed to shine at just the right moment.

"Yes. They got there five hours ahead just in case that happened."

Briggs was particularly nice with his smile today. "They get points for optimism."

I laughed. "They should be getting in this evening around five." Bear loped behind the counter to look for the treat jar. The massive puppy was quickly growing into his gargantuan paws and floppy ears. His spotted gray fur was taking on a nice silver sheen. He was a good looking dog. He looked extra wonderful next to his owner.

I headed to the treat jar that I kept filled with chicken flavored treats just for Bear. His wet nose twitched back and forth in the air before I even took off the lid. "It seems I'm going to be replaced as the smell expert soon." I gave Bear the treat.

"I don't think so. He's only interested if the smell leads to a treat." Another nice grin. This one a little lopsided. His usual five o'clock shadow was a few hours ahead of schedule. It always made him look just slightly roguish, especially with the crooked smile.

Briggs leaned against the work stool on the opposite side of the counter. He seemed less cool and confident than usual. But it wasn't agitation. Briggs was always a hard man to read. That came from being a detective.

He reached up and combed his fingers through his hair. "Are you planning to go to the fireworks show Wednesday night?" The question seemed to come out faster than he expected.

"Of course. It sounds fun." I leaned my forearms on the work island. "How about you? Or do you have to work?"

"Yes, no." He shook his head once. "I mean, yes, I was planning on going and no, I don't have to work." He stared at me over the work island for a few seconds. For that instant, I could almost convince myself that my theory of him not being interested was wrong.

"I was wondering—" he started. "Well, that is, if you don't already have a—" He stopped short of saying the word date. A twinge of disappointment grabbed me and held tightly. "What I'm asking . . . with all the eloquence of jabbering numbskull . . . is—I would love it if we could go together."

The phrase 'heart be still' circled my head a few seconds while I waited to make sure he didn't end it with a hearty laugh and a gotcha. Nope. His warm brown eyes waited with sparkling patience for my answer.

"I would like that, Detective Briggs." Right then, before the moment could be absorbed and analyzed too much, Bear hopped up on his back legs and clunked his big paws down on the counter. He panted hot breath toward Briggs.

"You're not invited," Briggs said. "Besides, you cower under the bed at thunder." He turned back to me with a profound look of concern. "I hadn't even thought about the noise from the fireworks show. Do you think he'll be all right?" In a few short months, Briggs had gone from an extremely reluctant dog owner to an overprotective dog parent. It was nothing short of adorable.

"You might ask the veterinarian if he can suggest something to help calm him. But if he's locked inside, I think he'll be all right." I quickly worried that he was having second thoughts about taking me to the fireworks show. "Of course, if you think you should stay home with Bear. I would understand."

Briggs' shoulders sank some. "No, not unless you've got someone else to go with?"

We sure were like-minded. "Nope, I'm free that night."

"Great. Sounds like a plan. I guess I better get back to the paperwork I've been putting off all day. Come on, Bear. You can annoy Hilda for awhile so I can get some work done." Briggs walked out with his giant sidekick trotting behind him.

I, of course, waited for them to be well out of sight before heading straight out the door and across the street to Lola's Antiques. Lola came out from the backroom as I stepped into the shop. She was wearing her favorite vintage Led Zeppelin t-shirt. I instantly noticed she had on more makeup than usual.

"Are you going somewhere?" I asked.

Her normally reddish lashes were black with mascara. She batted them in surprise. "No, why do you ask?"

"Well . . ." I pointed to my own face hoping it might jog her memory about the unusually heavy mascara and lipstick. "It's just that you're wearing makeup."

"So are you." She scooted behind the glass counter that

contained trays of vintage jewelry, antique lighters and every small bauble one might have worn in an earlier century.

"I'm not wearing that much," I protested far too abruptly, as if my dash of mascara was a crime. "Besides, I always wear it but you —" I flipped my hand. "Never mind. Not important." I cozied up to her counter. "I have something to tell you."

Her cocoa brown eyes glittered. "Me too. And my news will probably give you apoplexy."

I laughed. "Apoplexy? My friend, you have spent too many hours with your antiques. But I'll play along. I think my news might just give you the vapors, so we should probably move this chat to that old satin fainting couch in the corner." I was kidding but Lola liked the suggestion. Late Bloomer, Lola's elderly dog, was snoring at the foot of the fainting couch. Dust popped up from the worn satin upholstery as Lola and I sat, causing me to sneeze.

I rubbed my nose. "I swear I can still smell whatever Victorian perfume the owner of this couch was wearing when she rested on it. Violet, I think."

"Wow." Lola shook her head. "You're good. Or should I say, that nose is good. Violet was a Victorian favorite so you're probably right. When you die, that little super sniffer needs to be chopped off and hung in a museum or given to science."

I leaned back and pursed my lips at her suggestion.

"Sorry," Lola said. "My parents sent all these creepy antique medical school displays and teaching models they found in England. Guess I'm in sort of a macabre mood. Except, then something very un-macabre and cool happened at lunch. But you first. Oh wait. How was the garden club meeting? Does it have to do with that?"

I blew a puff of exasperated air from my lips. "Yes, that's it. We're going to sell herbs at the festival." I poked her shoulder. "See. Vapors, right?"

She stared at me for a second through one eye. "You're joking, aren't you?"

"Yes. Silly. The garden club meeting was interesting because there are some fascinating dynamics between the members, but I'll save that for another time because I've got to get back. Briggs came into the flower shop a few minutes ago. He asked me if I wanted to watch the fireworks show with him. And now, saying it out loud, it's just about as exciting as the herb sale." My posture sagged. "I think I'm reading too much into it. It's just fireworks."

"No, you're not. I'm not sure when or how it happened, but the fireworks show somehow morphed into a sort of romantic date thing. There will be families and chirpy little kids twittering about, but it's definitely considered a date if someone asks you." Lola pulled a rubber band out of her jean shorts and wrapped her thick red hair in a ponytail.

"I don't know. I'm feeling kind of deflated about the whole thing. He sort of made a point of avoiding the D word when he asked. I'm just so confused about our friendship. I mean, I've been in relationships, and as my mom will tell you, I've even broken off a perfectly good engagement for a trivial reason like him sneaking behind my back. I'm not a kid anymore, but I have absolutely no idea where I stand with Briggs. One minute, I think things are heading toward something serious and the next, I'm thinking I'm just a buddy that he likes to hang out with. Ugh, he's destroyed my confidence. I shouldn't even watch the fireworks with him."

Lola reached over and squeezed my face between her hands. "Snap out of it before I have to slap you. You're over-thinking everything. Just go, enjoy the show and see what happens."

I took a deep breath and sucked in some more ancient dust from the couch. I coughed into my fist and stood up to avoid the musty cloud. Lola hopped up too but Late Bloomer kept on snoring.

"What's your news?" I asked. "Wait, before you tell me, I'm

going to tell you something else. Only you can't tell the person I'm about to talk about. He'd be upset if he knew that I talked to you about this."

Lola tapped her chin. "Let me guess. You're going to say something about Ryder?" Her dry, sarcastic tone drowned my hopes that she'd take my suggestion but I forged ahead.

"I think you should ask Ryder to the fireworks show or at least hint to him that you don't have a date."

She lifted her chin. "How do you know I don't have a date? It just so happens I do."

"Do you? Oh poop. Ryder will be disappointed. Just let him down easy if he asks."

Lola grabbed the feather duster from the counter and began flipping it over the ornate shades on a pair of Victorian lamps. "A good, supportive friend would ask me who my date was before lecturing about how to politely reject someone."

"You're right, Lola. I guess I'm just worried about Ryder. So, who is the lucky man? And please don't let it be that weird, loud guy who works on the crab boat."

"Ick no. I thought he was cute for about four seconds. We never even met for that cup of coffee." She ran her feather duster across several bookshelves. It seemed she was drawing this out for dramatic effect.

"Well?" I said.

"I'm going with Ryder. He asked me earlier today."

I did the fast clap thing for a few seconds and then hugged her. One date, or possible date, and I was back in high school. This time it was the feather duster that caused me to sneeze. "This store and my sensitive nose are not a good match."

"Guess that says more about my shop keeping skills than your nose," she said. "Shouldn't you be leaving soon to pick your parents up at the airport?"

"I've been spared the long drive by my dad's urge to drive a

27

convertible along the coast. He rented a car for the vacation. I just hope they can find my house. They haven't exactly mastered the map app on the phone. Let's just say, they've been stranded in many a strange place because 'map lady' as my mom calls the voice, led them astray. Well, I've got to head back and finish planting herbs for the garden club booth."

Lola moved on to an antique hat rack where she'd hung some straw hats that were festooned with a broad red, white and blue ribbon. "Hey, maybe we should wear matching hats for the big evening." She was kidding, of course, but it reminded me of the stressful garden club meeting.

"Remind me to tell you about that garden club meeting and our dear friend Kate Yardley and her questionable business practices."

Lola's eyes rounded. "Now I've got to hear it. I'll definitely remind you."

I pushed open the door. "Later."

CHAPTER 5

A flashy blue Mustang convertible pulled into the driveway. I'd gone through every emotion, which included trepidation, horror and worry, waiting for my parents visit but now seeing them, looking excited, sporty and a touch sunburned in their rental car, I was thrilled about the visit.

Mom pushed her pearl white sunglasses higher on her nose and exited the sports car like she was just about to walk the red carpet. She'd let her natural silver gray start to take over her light brown hair. She'd had it cut short and chic and styled with a lot of whips, flips and turns, reminding me of the frosting on a cupcake. It must have been coated heavily with hairspray because the trip from the airport in the open car hadn't knocked one strand out of place. She was wearing one of six new t-shirts she'd bought for the trip. I'd received a flurry of pictures from her shopping adventure. Apparently, once she'd found the shirt she liked, she bought the same style in six different colors, one for each day of the visit. Today was magenta day.

Mom scurried to the front porch squealing all the way. It

seemed she was getting faster and more energetic with each passing year.

She stopped and put her hands on her hips to lob the first advice in a long string of unwanted advice nuggets, her specialty. "I think a new yellow coat of paint would spruce this place up."

"I agree but my wallet does not." We simultaneously threw open our arms for a hug.

Over her shoulder, I caught Dad struggling to get a heavy suitcase out of the trunk. "I'm going to help Dad. Go inside, Mom. There's some lemonade on the counter."

"Hmm, that sounds good. Convertibles are overrated," she said in a low voice, even though there was no way Dad could hear her over his symphony of grunts and curses.

"Dad, let me help." I reached the bottom step and wondered why I hadn't heard the screen door snap shut. Mom was standing at the screen staring cautiously inside.

"Kingston is in his cage," I called. "I warned him he was too scary for Grandma. His feelings are hurt, but I'll make it up to him with treats."

"A menacing black crow for a grandchild. What did I do wrong?" She scoffed to herself as she entered the house. I knew too well that by the time I walked inside with Dad, Mom would have memorized a list of changes that needed to be made to make my house more livable.

Dad's face was red from strain. He stopped his quest to free the heavy suitcase from the tiny trunk. "I think she packed bowling balls in this thing." Dad's face rolled up into his warm smile and we hugged. His hair had receded and his belly had proceeded (or whatever the opposite of receded was) since my last trip home at Christmas. He'd told me then that while other people worked to trim their tummies, he was working on a big belly because it would be the perfect ledge for the television remote.

I patted his belly. "Guess you're working hard toward that remote shelf, eh?"

"Yep, and now we've got that other thingamagoo for the subscription channels, so I need room for two remotes. Thanksgiving ought to do the trick."

I laughed and hugged him again. "It's so good to see you, Dad. Can't wait to introduce you to my new friends."

As if on cue, Dash pulled into his driveway. He waved at us. Dash and I had come to a friendship agreement after an awkward kiss attempt at Pickford Lighthouse. That uncomfortable moment was soon followed by a terrifying attack by a murderer. Both Dash and Briggs were nearby and saved me, then they tore into each other. Even after working together to do something heroic, (like saving the local flower shop owner) they were still ready to throw fists at each other. The source of the anger was still a mystery to me, but since Dash and I lived next door to each other, we decided to remain friends. I was relieved.

I motioned Dash over even though he was already heading our way. "Nice wheels," he commented and stuck out his hand. "I'm Dash, Lacey's neighbor. You must be Stanley Pinkerton. Nice to meet you."

"Since you're here, big strong neighborly fella—" I pointed to Mom's lead weighted suitcase that was jammed unhelpfully into a small trunk.

Dash did a short flex show of his arms before reaching in and plucking the case out as if it contained pillows.

The screen door popped open. My mom didn't have my super sense of smell but she could catch the scent of a handsome, eligible bachelor from a mile away. Or in this case, a small front room and eight foot wide porch away. She was a blur of magenta cotton as she sailed down the steps and across the lawn to the driveway.

"And this has to be the lovely Peggy Pinkerton." Dash kissed the back of her hand. The man had charm down to a magnificent art. I hated to tell him that he didn't need to try so hard. As long as you were tall, dark and single, you were a prince in my mom's book.

For obvious reasons, like one glaring magenta clad reason, I kept details about the men in my life to a minimum during our weekly mother-daughter chats. Mom nearly crumpled into a wilted ball of sobs when I told her I'd broken off my engagement to Jacob, the wealthy (philandering) heir to a perfume fortune. Ever since that heartbreak (hers more than mine) she'd taken it upon herself to find a suitable replacement. Fortunately for me, I lived a four hour flight from home, so she had to give up on the idea of playing matchmaker with various bridge club members' second cousins and single sons.

Dash carried the suitcase up the steps while Mom recuperated from the hand kiss. Dad followed right along with him telling him about the ride over in the Mustang. I followed behind with Mom. I could have pre-scripted her exact words long before she uttered them. She was that predictable.

Her hair moved with her head in one silver crown of hairspray as she tilted closer to whisper. "Oh wow, he sure is handsome. What did you say he did for a living?"

"He's a boat mechanic down in the marina."

I sensed her enthusiastic posture wilt some. "Oh well, I suppose some things can be overlooked."

I stopped short of the porch and kept my whisper low. "Yep and you can keep overlooking. We are just friends." Mom's footsteps pounded the wood porch steps just a little harder than necessary as we climbed up them and entered the house.

I had taken Elsie's blueberry dessert out of the refrigerator so it would be easier to cut. The rich, fruity scent of berries filled the air. The fragrance certainly had Kingston on alert. He slid back and forth along the perch in his cage, trying hard not to be insulted about being locked inside before bedtime.

"Stay for some refreshment, Dash," Mom offered quickly. She'd been in my house twenty seconds and had apparently stepped directly into the role of hostess. She hated not being hostess. More than once, I'd seen her take over my Aunt Rhonda's Thanksgiving feast so quickly and thoroughly, Rhonda ended up thanking Mom for the lovely meal and table settings as we left.

Mom turned her glittering eyes my way. "Why, sweetie, did you bake this? It's beautiful and smells delicious." She shook her head. "Lacey is so talented."

I winked at Dash. "Yes, it took an amazing amount of skill to drive Elsie's dessert home from the shop. Carried it in by myself and everything."

Thankfully Dad stopped the silly conversation. "Lacey, is this the same crow you've always had?"

Dash caught my arched brow and stifled a grin.

I walked to the cage. Kingston fluffed in anger and then fluttered his wings hard enough to cause my dad to take a step back.

"That's the same old, spoiled bird, Kingston. Should I let him out so you can give him a treat?" Right then, Kingston turned his menacing beak toward my dad and favored him with one of his crow death stares.

"Some other time, Lacey. It's been a long day. I think I'll have some of that lemonade."

Dash touched my arm and motioned for me to follow him out to the porch. "Nice meeting you both. I'm sure we'll see more of each other this week."

Mom's face dropped like a failed cheese soufflé. "But aren't you going to stay? I'm sure this Elsie woman baked a wonderful dessert." My earlier notion that Mom would quickly bond with Elsie deflated just like her face. I'd told Mom about Elsie and her baking talents many times.

"Another time," Dash said. "My dog will be waiting for his dinner."

I walked out to the porch with him. "Did I exaggerate?" I asked.

"You did not. But I like them both."

"Well, that shine might wear off when Mom brings you a catalog for groom tuxes. In case you need one, wink wink, nod nod."

Dash laughed. "That's why I wanted to talk to you outside. I know this is late notice, but I was wondering if you'd go with me to Wednesday night's firework show? We don't have to call it a date. I know. You've made it clear that we are just friends. But it has somehow morphed into a couples' thing, and I find myself without a couple. Or, more clearly, you're the woman I'd like to sit and do 'ooos and awws' with."

He finished his long invitation, but I was still not solid on how to answer. Guess the simple truth was always best. "Dash, I've already got a date. A couple. A person to—You get it."

Dash's green eyes showed a hint of hurt. "I guess I should've figured you were going with Briggs. I was just assuming that Detective Bah Humbug would be skipping the holiday."

I tilted my head and peered up at him to show my disapproval.

"Right. Sorry, Lacey. I'll see you later. Have fun with your visitors." He was working hard to keep the disappointment out of his tone.

"Drop by later for a piece of Elsie's dessert. I'm sure you'll be able to taste all of my talents through her Blueberry Delight." Humor was my go to tactic whenever the conversation between us got sticky. It usually worked but not tonight.

Even Dash's Hollywood smile was less dazzling as he walked away.

CHAPTER 6

The smell of bacon was so powerful it woke me from a deep sleep. Before opening my eyes or lifting my head from the pillow, I kicked my feet back and forth under the covers to feel for Nevermore's weighty body. No cat. Super sleuth that I was, I quickly connected the cat's mysterious disappearance to the bacon aroma.

I rubbed my eyes and squinted into the daylight coming down the hallway. Mom must have performed her 'open the windows and let the world in' routine. It was a habit that made me cringe in high school. I'd be buried deeply in some teenage dream only to have my mom throw open my bedroom curtains to 'let the world in'. Unfortunately, with the way my room was positioned, the world also meant blinding early morning sunshine.

I picked up my phone to find out why the alarm hadn't gone off. I quickly discovered the reason. I still had another half hour of blissful sleep. I pulled on my robe and padded down the hallway on bare feet. The sound of my dad's voice and bacon sizzling on the frying pan instantly transported me back to my childhood. I'd wake up on Sunday and hurry to the kitchen where Mom would be preparing breakfast and Dad would be leaning over the Sunday paper grousing about the terrible world news.

I reached my kitchen. Only my mom would remember to pack one of her hundred multi-colored aprons for a vacation. Nevermore was sitting obediently at her feet waiting for fate to step in and drop a piece of egg or bacon his way. Dad was standing in the front room giving Kingston a treat. The only newspaper beneath him was the paper lining Kingston's cage.

Dad was beaming proudly as he said good morning. "Hey, kiddo, I think your bird really likes me." Kingston danced as Dad reached into the treat can and pulled out another peanut butter flavored dog snack. Kingston took it greedily and carried it to his favorite part of the perch to eat it. Dad reached for another treat.

"Wait, Dad, how many of those have you given him?"

Dad shrugged. "Haven't been counting."

I walked over and took the can from him. "If you have to use the word counting in your answer, then he's already had too many. He'll be twittering and chattering like a kid on the morning after Halloween."

Dad laughed. "Can birds get sugar highs?"

"Not sure about birds." I put the lid on the can to assure Kingston his morning of glorious gluttony had ended. "But Kingston stopped being a bird when he started insisting that he eat his cereal from a bowl."

"Breakfast is ready," Mom called from her—uh, my kitchen. She placed plates on my tiny kitchen table that were piled so high with eggs, bacon and biscuits, I worried about the legs on my wobbly, little table.

Mom caught my hesitation. "Sit down and eat, Lacey. You look thin. I'll bet it's been a long time since you've had a home-cooked meal."

"Unless you count all the meals I make myself . . . here . . . at home. And besides, I'm not skinny. My shop is right next to Elsie's bakery. She brings me goodies and samples all day."

Dad adjusted his pants that were now buckled beneath his round waist before sitting to his plate. "That berry dessert was sure delicious."

Mom shrugged and made a sort of puffy sound. "I mean, you can't really go wrong with cream cheese and syrup glazed berries."

"Mom," I said with an exaggerated sigh. "You haven't met Elsie, but it seems you've already formed an opinion of her." I poured myself a glass of juice.

Dad shoveled a forkful of eggs into his mouth but that didn't stop him from talking. "Your mom—" He chewed quickly and swallowed. "Your mom is jealous of Elsie because they are the same age but you spend much more time with Elsie than her. She thinks she's been replaced."

Mom crossed her arms and blinked hard at Dad. He just kept eating, ignoring the laser eyed glare being pointed his direction. "If I'd wanted to tell her that, Stanley, I would have told her myself."

"Mom, I spend more time with her because you are in a different state, and Elsie is literally fifty steps away in her bakery. She's a good friend, yes. But you're my mom *and* good friend. So you have two titles. She only has one."

"Unless you count best baker," Dad added unhelpfully as he smeared butter on his biscuit.

I tapped his foot to let him know he had once again earned a scowl. Dad looked up and smiled. "But of course, you are best baker too, Peg. So that gives you three titles."

"Stan, shut up and eat your breakfast." Mom picked up her napkin and placed it on her lap. "Thank you, Lacey. That's very nice of you to say."

"Just give Elsie a chance, Mom. I think you'll like her." I picked up a piece of bacon. "What are you two sporty, top down travelers going to do today? Cruise the coast?"

Mom stopped halfway to her biscuit. "We thought we might just shop around town. Check out your store. See what you're up to."

I knew my chin had dropped onto the table but I couldn't seem to lift it back up.

Dad laughed. "You got her good, Peggy."

Mom smiled and took a bite.

"Phew. Not that I mind having you guys hang around," I said quickly.

Mom reached for her juice. "Relax, sweetie. We aren't going to get in the way of your life while we're here. Not too much, anyhow." She followed that declaration with her next prying question. "When will we meet the elusive mysterious detective you talk so much about?"

After the ridiculous matchmaker show Mom put on in front of Dash the night before, I was looking less forward to introducing her to Briggs. But I was sure the moment was unavoidable. For now, there were always stalling tactics. "Detective Briggs is always very busy, Mom. He covers this whole stretch of coast and for such small towns there always seems to be some kind of mayhem taking place. From my experience, there could be foul play or even a murder at any moment." The last came from a touch of grim wishful thinking. I loved a good mystery but things had been pretty calm since spring when a promising artist was murdered near the Pickford Lighthouse.

Dad stopped vacuuming the breakfast long enough to talk. "You know, I think I'd really like to see that Hawksville place you told us about at Christmas."

Mom rolled her eyes. "I guess we know where you inherited that ghoulish curiosity from."

"Ghoulish? That's an adjective I never expected to hear my own mom use about me." I turned to Dad. "It's actually Hawksworth.

And we can walk up there later to satisfy our ghoulish cravings." I winked at him.

"Perfect." Dad slathered more butter on his biscuit.

I finished a piece of bacon and discretely handed Nevermore a bit of egg. I downed one biscuit that was dripping in butter, but I'd reached my capacity. I never ate a lot in the morning. "Mom, this breakfast is delicious but I can't eat all of this. I'm riding my bicycle to work. I'm pretty sure I won't make it if I'm filled with all this food."

"But all those eggs will go to waste," Mom lamented. "I know, I'll put them between some toast and mayonnaise and top the whole thing with fresh tomatoes. You can eat it for lunch. It'll be like having an egg salad sandwich." She stood right up to proceed with her plan. "I wonder if Elsie is clever enough to think of a second use for scrambled eggs?"

"It's only a sandwich, Peggy. Not a cure for cancer." Dad snuck me a wink. "Guess you'll be just as glad to see the backside of us when we head home," Dad muttered quietly over his cup of coffee.

I reached over and squeezed his arm. "Nonsense. I love seeing you both. Have fun today and try not to get lost."

"Yeah, tell that to the 'crazy map lady' in my phone."

CHAPTER 7

$\mathcal{A}$ drifty, fast moving coastal fog was just receding from the town as I rolled up to the flower shop on my bicycle. The damp air gave an extra kick to my already curly hair. I was trying to tame an overexcited ringlet when I ran into Kate Yardley as she headed toward Elsie's Sugar and Spice Bakery. Kate was the fashion icon of the town. And while I'd at least taken the time to splash on some mascara to go with my pink t-shirt and shorts, Kate was dressed, styled and made up for a walk down a runway. The adorable mini sailor dress she wore had big brass buttons and a cute blue collar. Kate transformed her appearance from day to day but she always looked edgy and cool. Even today, with the red, white and blue stripes in her bangs. I, on the other hand, had my own ridiculous Shirley Temple look going.

My usual confidence always took a dive whenever I came face to face with Kate. And it seemed that was about to happen. Kate headed past Elsie's stylish and totally impractical sidewalk furniture to the sidewalk in front of my shop.

I quickly pushed my unruly locks behind my ears in an attempt to look less clownish. "Morning, Kate. You're out and about early."

Kate smiled primly, not wanting to appear too friendly, apparently. "I had an urge for one of Elsie's blueberry muffins. I'm sure I'll regret it." She ran her hands down along her waist and hips to remind me that she had a great figure. (Not that I needed the reminder.) "I'll deal with the guilt after the last crumb is gone."

"You have strong self-control, Kate. That's why you always look fabulous." The one thing I'd learned about Kate was it was always better to give sugar instead of salt in any conversation. The woman could be slightly venomous if given the chance, but flattery always softened her fangs. "Well, I should get inside." I pointed my thumb over my shoulder.

"Has anyone asked you to the fireworks show?" Kate blurted before I could peel away. We were certainly not in the kind of friendship where it could be considered an appropriate or expected question. But I knew she was asking because she had a major thing for my neighbor, Dash. Apparently, in pre-Pink history, namely the time before my arrival, Dash and Kate had been dating. It had ended, at least according to Dash. Kate still seemed on the fence about it.

I favored her with a forced smile. "Why, as a matter of fact, yes."

Kate parted her heavily glossed lips expectantly, waiting for me to fill in details. But I'd given my answer. She didn't need to know who I was going to the festival with. I was sure she'd prod me more, but the whole conversation was cut short when Jenny walked out of the bakery and curtly called Kate's name.

"Miss Yardley, Kate." Jenny was pointing her librarian's finger as she walked toward us.

"Oh brother," Kate muttered under her breath.

Jenny nodded good morning to me and then returned her angry gaze to Kate. I was slightly taken aback. I'd never seen Jenny anything but sweet and amicable. I definitely would not have wanted to talk too loudly in her library. It seemed the scene on the sidewalk was about to get interesting. I knew exactly why Jenny looked so angry and since her ire was pointed at Kate, I made a slow process of parking my bicycle in front of the shop so I could eavesdrop. I wasn't proud of my plan but that didn't stop me.

"You specifically told me that the patriotic hat I purchased was one of a kind," Jenny said. "Then my friend Molly walked into a garden club meeting with the same hat. Apparently, you sold her the same bill of goods, telling her it was one of a kind. So you lied to both of us."

I stooped to check the tire pressure on my bike. Of course I had no idea what that meant, a tire was either flat or it wasn't, but I gave them both a good squeeze to make it look official while I waited for Kate's response. With the exception of whenever Dash was nearby, Kate was always cool as a cucumber. This morning was no different, even facing down an angry customer.

"I didn't lie. If you took the time to check each hat carefully, you'd see that the hat Molly purchased has smaller silver star studs and your hat has two extra rhinestones on the brim. So they are one of a kind."

Jenny's tongue was caught in disbelief. I couldn't blame her.

Kate waved at her and sashayed past, deciding she'd won the argument by silencing her opponent.

I was just about to walk up and pat Jenny on the back to snap her out of her stunned silence but she found her tongue first. "You are a deceptive saleswoman. I will not step foot in your store again. And I'll make sure to let all my friends know too."

Kate disappeared into the bakery without even a cursory glance back.

Jenny swung around to me. Her cheeks were dark pink. "Can you believe that?"

I shook my head. "I'm sorry that happened, Jenny. And I agree.

Very deceptive. But it's not anything to let ruin your day. By the way, I'm almost done with the herb pots."

The new, much more agreeable topic seemed to help cool her down. "Terrific. We'll be setting up in the last booth before the lighthouse lawn. It's a little out of the way, but we snagged a spot under the sprawling mulberry so there'll be some shade."

"Great. I'll bring the pots by later. And, Jenny, try and have a good day."

"Thanks, Lacey. I will."

Ryder had volunteered to open up the shop, thinking I'd be in late because of my parents' visit. Instead, the opposite happened and I was a little early.

Ryder popped out of the back holding a patriotic bouquet of white daisies, blue stocks and mini red roses. "You're here. Uh oh, trouble with Ma and Pa Pinkerton?"

I laughed. "No, Ma and Pa are good. But they wanted to get an early start on their day."

Ryder leaned to look past the bouquet and me. "Where's Kingston?"

"My dad fed him too many treats this morning. When I opened the cage to shoo him out, he just crouched on his perch looking like my Uncle Robert after his third piece of pumpkin pie. Kingston needs to—as they say—sleep it off."

I walked to the back to put my egg sandwich in the refrigerator before getting back to work on the herbs. Elsie strode in just as I returned to the shop front. She had her lips turned in as if she had a ripe, plum morsel of information to tell me.

"Spill it, Elsie. Before your head explodes."

Elsie bustled forward, like only she could. "Jenny came into the shop this morning." She waved her hand quickly. "Never mind, I know you saw her because the two of you were talking on the sidewalk. Anyhow, she told me in strictest confidence—"

A short laugh shot from my mouth. "Which is why you

marched straight over to fill me in on every juicy detail."

My sarcastic comment didn't faze her for a moment. "Exactly. Anyhow, Jenny is the main judge for the Fourth of July pie contest. She chooses Molly every year because, frankly, there just aren't that many good pies entered. I suppose Carla's lemon meringue is pretty good but anyway, I'm trailing off on a pie tangent. Well, Jenny told me she suspected that Molly might have been entering a prebaked pie each year."

I rubbed my brows trying to figure out what she meant. "As opposed to a raw pie?"

"No, silly. I mean a pie that she purchased from a bakery and then placed in one of her own pie plates to make it look as if it came right out of her very own kitchen."

"So Molly has been entering a professional baker's pie. Is it one of yours?"

Elsie patted my arm to assure me I was being silly again. "No, of course not. Everyone in town knows when they're eating one of my pies."

I laughed. "The baker said humbly. But you're right. Jenny would be able to recognize one of your pies. How does she know for sure?"

"I guess she doesn't yet but she's working on it so she can disqualify Molly from the contest."

I spread my mouth wide. "Whoa, sounds like it could get messy between those two."

"You wanted to be a member of the club," Elsie reminded me. "How did your parents like the dessert and when do we get to meet them?"

"They loved it, of course." I thought about Mom's underwhelming assessment, which had more to do with the baker than the dessert. I had no choice but to introduce Elsie to Mom, but I wasn't looking forward to it.

I forced a smile. "You'll be meeting them soon."

CHAPTER 8

*R*yder was whistling every tune he could remember as he finished putting together yellow rose centerpieces for a party. He was always in a good mood, but this morning he was exceptionally happy. I was only guessing but something told me it had to do with Lola going with him to the fireworks show.

"Someone has taken up the Seven Dwarves mantra of whistling while you work," I said as I placed tiny pots of rosemary in a box.

"Yep, it's that kind of a morning. Sun is shining. I've got a great boss and I love my job."

I bowed to him as a thank you. "That's all very nice to hear, but I'm thinking your mood might have something to do with the red haired, rock 'n' roll loving antique peddler across the lane."

Ryder lifted a glass vase of yellow roses to make sure it was even on all sides. "Yes, you could be right about that." He put the vase down and patted his pocket. "And I've got my money all ready for the picnic basket auction."

"Oh, are you planning on buying a basket? That's nice. I heard the town council uses the money to spruce up the town square during the holidays."

"I'm not planning to buy *a* basket. I'm going to buy Lola's. It's sort of part of the tradition to buy the basket of the person you've asked to the festival."

I dropped the last pot of rosemary on the floor, but the tiny plant managed to stay tucked in place. I stooped down. As I swept stray dirt back into the pot, I jumped back in my memory to look for a mention, any mention of Lola's basket. I couldn't recall that scenario, and knowing Lola as well as I did, I was sure she had no intention of making one. Nor did I, for that matter.

I pushed back to my feet. "So, if Detective Briggs asked me to the fireworks show, then there's a good chance that he expects to buy my basket?"

"I'd say so. I mean Detective Briggs doesn't always participate in our quaint town traditions, but he might be planning on it."

I plopped the last pot into the box. "Oh dear. I'll be right back, Ryder." I hurried to the office to grab my wallet and headed to the door.

"I take it you're going to the Corner Market to buy picnic basket items," he said.

"Nothing gets past you, buddy." I pushed out the door and glanced back into the window to make sure Ryder's focus was on his work. Then I shot across the street and into Lola's shop. I found her between customers, perusing a magazine at the counter.

"Grab some cash, friend. We've got shopping to do at Corner Market."

Her brows were scrunched as she glanced up. "I'm good. I just bought groceries yesterday."

"Nope you're not good. Unless you've already prepared your picnic basket for the auction."

She laughed and returned her attention to the magazine. "I

don't participate in that outdated and, sexist, I might add, tradition."

I walked to the counter and took hold of her wrist. "You do this year because Ryder has his cash and his bid ready to go. He's waiting to buy a basket. *Your* basket, to be exact."

She stared wide-eyed at me across the glass counter to see if I was kidding. I wasn't.

"Ugh," she groaned and took heavy stomping steps toward her office. "I don't even know what to put in one of those baskets."

"That makes two of us." I headed to the door to wait for her.

She returned still wearing her invisible, lead-filled shoes.

"Oh, cheer up," I said. "Besides, Ryder will be happy with a few granola bars and a premade tuna sandwich as long as it comes in your basket. Oh wait, do you have baskets? Something tells me Corner Market will be sold out."

Lola sighed. "I've got a few we can use. I'll just have to wipe the centuries of dust out of them."

I pushed open the door and then put my hand up abruptly, accidentally smacking her in the chest.

"Ouch."

"Sorry about that. Let me first scan my shop window to see if Ryder is in view. I told him I was going out to buy stuff for my basket but he was already certain you had yours filled. You know, in anticipation of him bidding on it." I squinted across the street. The glare on the front window made it hard to tell, but I didn't see any tall heads in view. "Coast is clear. Let's roll."

CHAPTER 9

I made Lola cross the street after we passed the flower shop. I decided to avoid walking directly past the police station. If Briggs was expecting to buy my picnic basket, I certainly didn't want him knowing that I was just putting the thing together hours before the evening auction. It was important that he knew I put a lot of thought into my embarrassingly thoughtless basket.

As we crossed Franki's Diner parking lot, Lola elbowed me and motioned with her head toward the entrance of the pier. Kate Yardley was standing on the first step talking to none other than my neighbor, Dash. She was pinching the skirt of her cute little sailor dress and tilting her head sweetly as she peered up at him through red, white and blue bangs.

"I'd love to be a pigeon on the pier to hear that conversation," Lola quipped.

I decided not to mention Dash's invitation to the fireworks show. Lola usually ran off with that kind of information and made it into something much bigger than it deserved.

"Let's concentrate on our picnic baskets. Then I'll tell you about Kate and her shady business practices."

My earlier prediction that the Corner Market would be sold out of baskets was correct. Unfortunately, they'd also sold out of a lot of the prepackaged snack foods like chips and granola bars. Lola and I had started our baskets too late. In our defense, we hadn't realized we were making them until a few minutes earlier.

Gigi Upton, who co-owned the store with her husband Tom, was stacking some apples in the produce stand. Her dachshunds Molly and Buddy were stretched out at her feet. Today she had them dressed in stars and stripes t-shirts. Just like Kate was the human fashion icon for the town, Molly and Buddy were Port Danby's canine trendsetters.

After seeing Kate with Dash on the pier, I wondered if the two of them were firming up plans for a date to the fireworks show. Maybe Kate would be slipping into the market any moment to buy food for a last minute basket too. I stretched up to peer over the bread display. The front window afforded a great view of the pier. They were still chatting.

I headed to the lunch meats, deciding I was going to need to come up with some sort of sandwich idea. Lola had gone straight to the ready-made sandwiches and salads supplied to Corner Market by a local deli.

"Oh man," Lola whined from the back of the store. "Even the deli stuff is all gone." Lola came around the corner. "That's it. Ryder is getting a gourmet basket of cold Pop Tarts and marshmallows."

I pulled a package of sliced peppered turkey from the refrigerator section. "Look, we can buy the stuff to make turkey and cheese sandwiches. There's no reason why we can't make identical baskets. Somehow, I don't picture Ryder and Briggs comparing notes."

"Good idea. Choose the cheese and I'll go pick some bread.

Hopefully, there will be more than just cinnamon raisin and gluten free on the shelf."

There were still enough cheeses left to make the decision process lengthy. It seemed cheddar was my safest bet but then a nice slice of jalapeno jack cheese might spice things up some. But was I ready for spicing things up? I stifled a laugh, not wanting to look too nutty chortling in the cheese refrigerator.

Cellophane crackled behind me. Lola startled me by tapping me on the shoulder.

"Wow, the bread announced itself, but I didn't hear you walk up." I glanced down at the loaf of rye bread. "That's a good choice for turkey. I've got the meat and cheese. Let's get some tomatoes and red onion. The guys are going to be impressed with our culinary skills." I realized as I was rambling on about the sandwiches, Lola's attention had been diverted to the front of the store. She leaned right and left to get a look at something or someone between the grocery aisles.

"Who are you spying on?" I asked.

Lola shook her head. "I'm not." She hopped up on tiptoes to get a better look at her focal point.

"Then why are you doing ballet in the back of the store?"

She finally pulled her gaze from whatever was holding her interest. She leaned closer. "Check out the woman at the produce stand. I've never seen her before. She's really pretty."

I decided to humor her and peered around the display of dishwashing detergent. A woman, late twenties or early thirties, was smelling a cantaloupe. Lola was right. The woman had glowing golden skin, auburn hair and even from the distance I was standing, I could see that her eyes were bright blue.

I turned back to Lola and shrugged. "I'm sure she came in on one of those nice luxury boats in the marina. Probably in town for the fireworks show. I need to get back to the shop. Let's get the produce and check out."

The pretty stranger was still making her melon selection when we reached the tomatoes. She smiled briefly our way. I returned a polite nod. I searched for the reddest, ripest tomato, something to add a pop of sweet color to the sandwich. The onions and garlic in the next bin were intruding on my selection. Every tomato smelled like a bottle of spaghetti sauce.

"Oh, for heaven's sakes," Lola huffed as she picked up a large beefsteak tomato. "It's just a picnic basket. Not a culinary contest."

"Fine," I said with an insulted chin lift.

The attractive woman had chosen her melon, but as she walked past the front windows of the store something outside caught her eye. It was hard to know for sure, but it seemed she was watching the conversation between Dash and Kate. Dash was extremely handsome but even so, it seemed like an oddly long gaze for a stranger. It was almost as if she knew him. Before she turned away from the window, her brilliant blue gaze traveled across the street to the police station where it lingered for an odd amount of time.

"Is that all?" Gigi's question pulled me from my spy session. She circled behind the register. Molly came right up for a pat, but Buddy headed to the pillow behind the counter.

"Yep, this is it." I showed my wallet to Lola. "I've got this since you were a reluctant picnic maker, and I basically forced you into it."

Gigi smiled at our conversation. "You girls started this kind of late. Most of the gourmet goodies were bought up last week." She pulled out a paper bag to pack the food. "Let me know if you need help with anything," she called to the pretty woman. She had made her way back to the refrigerator section.

"Thanks, I will."

Lola leaned over the counter to whisper. "Who is she?"

Gigi shrugged. "I'm not sure but there is something familiar about her. Maybe she visits Port Danby every summer." She handed us the receipt and the bag. "Have fun. Sorry we don't have any more baskets."

"We've got that covered," I said. "Thanks, Gigi."

Lola and I hurried out of the store. The conversation on the pier had ended. Dash had gone back to work. Kate was heading toward Corner Market.

"Maybe she's going in to buy her picnic for Dash," Lola suggested.

"Maybe." I wasn't sure how I felt about Dash going to the celebration with Kate. Not sure why it bothered me but it did. And boy oh boy, was my mom going to be frowning in disappointment when she saw them together under the fireworks display.

CHAPTER 10

As luck would have it, Mom and Dad arrived at the shop just in time for Miss Hostess Supreme to put together my picnic basket. Of course she grumbled about the lack of pretty linen napkins and proper condiments while she created her divine looking sandwich. But then it wouldn't be Mom if there wasn't a grumble or two.

Les came over from the Coffee Hutch with complimentary mocha lattes for everyone. He and Dad hit it off instantly and quickly retired to the wonderful pub style seating in front of the Coffee Hutch to firm up details for a fishing trip. My dad heard the word fishing and stars, or maybe it was starfish, filled his eyes. It was no surprise to me that the two men got along immediately. My stomach was still in flutters, waiting for the big introduction. Elsie was busy in the bakery and hadn't had time to stop by.

"You'd think she could find a few minutes just to say hello," Mom muttered quietly as she cut some red, white and blue ribbon from the spools.

I finished the last calculation on a flower order and put my pen down. "She is running a busy bakery all by herself, Mom."

"Why doesn't she get a nice helper like Ryder?"

"I told you he was awesome. I'm sure if Elsie could find someone with all of Ryder's attributes, she'd hire the person instantly. He's just one of a kind."

Mom and Dad met Ryder before he took off for his break. They were both impressed. It was hard not to be with Ryder. He knew how to talk to everyone. Easy confidence came naturally to him in every situation and with everyone, save one person. Lola. His self-assurance just seemed to disappear whenever my best friend was near. I was hopeful that their relationship would start to blossom.

I carried my receipt book into the backroom. The shop bell rang. My mom stepped right out of picnic preparer and into flower shop saleswoman.

"How can we help you?" she asked whoever had walked inside.

"You must be Peggy," Elsie said.

I froze in my little office and listened with horror for my mom's reply. "Be nice, Mom," I said to myself. I quickly contemplated rushing out there but then my cowardly side suggested I just hide in the office.

I startled from Mom's sudden outburst.

"Oh my, you must be Elsie!" She was basically yelling. "Wow, you are so fit and trim. I'm so envious. Lacey told me you run all the time. I wish I could work up that kind of willpower. I'd be running all over the place. Maybe even entering marathons." Mom's gushing hello bordered on hysteria.

I finally got my coward's feet moving and headed out to the front of the shop to save Elsie. Her face made it clear that she was slightly stunned by Mom's over-the-top welcome. I quickly took the tray of brownies from her hands to make sure nothing happened to them. (Priorities and all that.)

Mom was pelting a dumbstruck Elsie with questions about the

right running shoes for older women and the best way to get started on a running regimen.

"Mom. Mom." It took me several more 'moms' to get her attention. "Let me introduce you properly. Then maybe you could couch the million questions about running for another time." I knew Mom was about as likely to start a running program as Dad was to start a sewing club. Wasn't going to happen, no matter how many questions she asked about it to make it seem possible.

"Mom, Peggy," I added. "This is my dear friend, Elsie. Elsie this is my mom, Peggy."

Elsie finally caught her breath from the enthusiastic welcome. "Nice to meet you, Peggy. I've heard so much about you. Let me just say we all just adore Pink, uh, I mean Lacey."

"Oh don't worry about that. Lacey's friends always called her Pink. I suppose that's why she named the shop Pink's Flowers." Mom was talking several times faster than normal, and there was a distinctive, high pitch in her tone. She was trying too hard. I tried to sneak her an expression to let her know that she could settle down, but she'd worked herself into a touch of frenzy.

"Thank you for the dessert," I interjected. "It was delicious. And these brownies smell divine. My dad loves fudge brownies."

"Yes, that dessert was fabulous," Mom piped up. "I've made something similar for our town block party, only I used raspberries and real whipped cream." She emphasized real.

Elsie smiled weakly, seemingly unsure how to respond. "Where is your dad? I'd love to meet him."

"He went next door with Les. They are planning a fishing trip," I answered quickly.

"I don't know what I'll do while your dad is off fishing," Mom said, sounding like a petulant child.

Before I could answer, Elsie stepped in and turned the whole bizarre first meeting into something fantastic. "Peggy, have you ever made petit fours?"

Mom shuffled in place on her new sandals. Today she was wearing a bright yellow t-shirt. It was a little hard on the eyes. "I have made them a few times at Christmas. They are a lot of work."

"I haven't made any since my early days in a French bakery, but I was thinking of trying it again. I would love your assistance. Maybe we can plan it on the same day as the fishing trip."

Mom looked close to tears. Tears of joy. "Only if you have time. I wouldn't want to get in your way. I know you have a busy day and so much work to do." She was gushing again, only this time it didn't sound extravagant and forced. Mom was genuinely thrilled at the prospect. And now, my adoration for Elsie was sealed. She'd turned an awkward moment upside down with her invitation.

"I have all the time in the world for the woman responsible for this dear girl." Elsie wrapped her arm around my shoulder for a squeeze. Now it seemed Elsie was pouring it on a bit thick, but it seemed we'd gotten past the initial meeting and it was a huge success. As long as they didn't spend their petit four bake session discussing and organizing my love life. The thought of them alone talking about the one person they had in common terrified me some, but I'd get over it. I was just glad to see Mom happy.

"While you two decide on the baking day details, I've got to haul these herbs down to the marina."

"I've got to get back to the bakery." Elsie headed to the door. "Besides, we need to see what day Les and your dad pick for fishing."

"Nice meeting you and thank you for the brownies," Mom called as Elsie walked out. Mom turned to me with her big Cheshire cat grin. "What a lovely woman." She plucked a brownie from the tray and took a bite. "And such a great baker."

I patted my belly. "You don't have to tell me, Mom." I picked up the first box of herbs. Dad had driven the convertible to the shop. He'd left me the keys to drive the plants down to the pier.

Since tomorrow was a holiday, I decided to shut the shop down early. I needed to get the herbs to the garden club booth and my meticulously planned and prepared picnic basket to the auction. Naturally, I planned to confess to Briggs that my mom was the artist behind the sandwich. Unless maybe I forgot, which might happen too. Another thought suddenly dampened my spirit. What if he was too busy to bother with the auction? What if my lonely basket was left behind because no one wanted to bid on it? Why were holidays in this town so darn stressful?

Dad saw me loading the trunk of the car. He quickly finished his coffee and joined me. "Do you need some help, sport?"

"Yeah, Dad, there's just one more box. I need to grab the picnic basket."

We walked back into the flower shop. Mom was doing what she loved doing. Straightening and organizing. When she'd first walked into the shop, she'd had only one criticism—that the place looked a 'touch chaotic'. I assured her it was because Ryder and I had been too busy to clean up cuttings and petals and ribbons shreds. Otherwise, she seemed impressed and that was good enough for me. It seemed I owed Ryder a piece of pie.

"Do you want me to drive you?" Dad asked. "I could help you deliver herbs."

Mom placed the ribbon spool she'd been rewinding back on the dowel. "Let's all go, Stan. I'd like to take a walk on the beach."

CHAPTER 11

he scene at the park was hectic but festive. Colorful red, white and blue paper pinwheels dangled from the marina lights. Strings of star shaped bulbs were hung along the shops on the pier and tiny flags were waving everywhere. My parents had headed out for their walk along the beach. They really seemed to be enjoying themselves.

I helped Jenny finish setting up the garden club booth. We fought the afternoon coastal breeze the entire time but managed to finally anchor our garden club sign to the table with large stones. The herbs I donated were still small enough that they stood easily in their teeny pots waiting to be taken to their new homes.

Jenny adjusted her rhinestone hat to keep the sun off her face as she ran through her check off sheet.

"Shouldn't Molly be here helping?" I asked. Of course, I hadn't mentioned the whole bakery pie scandal to Jenny. Elsie had told me in confidence, and I certainly didn't want to step into the center of a sticky situation.

"Molly always finds excuses to avoid helping," Jenny said with a head shake. "Sometimes, I don't know why she bothers to be a member. All she ever does is complain and hurt Carla's feelings."

"Yes, I noticed some tension there."

Jenny elbowed me discretely. "Speaking of Carla. Here she comes with her husband, Vernon." Jenny spoke quickly to fill me in. "Every year, Vernon bids on my picnic basket. We both grew up in the same region in Georgia. Vernon says my fried chicken tastes just like his mom's. Carla gets so mad but that doesn't stop him. Guess my chicken is worth a few days of ice from the wife. And that woman is always so suspicious and jealous. She thinks everyone is after Vernon. Can't tell you how often she's told me she thought there was funny business going on between other women and her husband. I'd like to be honest and tell her no one would be interested but I don't want to be mean."

I squinted across the way to the oddly matched couple walking toward us. Vernon was indeed, much shorter and slighter than his wife. He had a full head of red hair and skin that was white as powder and dotted with freckles. His pale skin had a slightly cadaverous glow which looked almost blue in the sunlight. "Why does he—"

"Look like a shiny corpse?" Jenny asked. She spoke quickly again. "A special prescription sun block for his fair skin." Jenny straightened and raised the volume on her voice. "Carla, Vernon, I wondered where you guys were."

Carla smiled at me. "Lacey, this is my husband, Vernon."

He nodded politely and reached out his hand. My nose was instantly overtaken by the strong smell of sun block. Only instead of the usual fruity fragrance, this one smelled like vanilla.

Vernon did seem to have a leering stare to go with a somewhat creepy grin. Maybe Carla's suspicions weren't that far off.

"Ladies and gentlemen," Mayor Price's booming voice thundered through an auctioneer's microphone. "We are about start the picnic basket auction. Please make your way to the stand."

I glanced around for familiar faces and saw Ryder walking toward the auction. My parents were heading up the steps at the far side of the pier. No sign of Lola, or, more importantly, my basket buyer. It seemed my prediction that Briggs wouldn't bother to stop by for the auction was coming true. How humiliating it would be to have no one buy my basket and right in front of the mayor. I was sure that would make his day.

I peeled off from the rest of the crowd and stood closer to the steps that led to the beach, thinking I could make a quick, humiliated exit if necessary. The auction started with Jenny's basket. Mayor Price started the bids off at five dollars, but Vernon ended it quickly with his twenty dollar bid. I had to hand it to the guy, he was standing in the glowering shadow of a wife who looked like she could pound him into the ground with a few good thwacks on the head, but he still bought the basket. Jenny pressed her hand to her chest in feigned surprise as if she wasn't expecting it.

Then came the part I hadn't expected. Jenny walked forward with her basket, took hold of Vernon's proffered arm and the two wandered off to eat the meal.

"What on earth?" I asked myself quietly.

"What on earth what?" Lola chirped from behind. She had dressed for the occasion by replacing her faded vintage Led Zeppelin shirt with a newer Rolling Stones tee. She'd pushed an olive green fedora down over her thick hair for another touch of class.

I motioned toward Jenny and Vernon, who were heading down to the beach with their fried chicken. "The person who buys the basket then eats with the basket filler?" I asked.

"What did you think?"

"Uh, that they took the thing back to their car or wherever and ate it in solitude. Now my basket is going to look extra pathetic when it's left behind on the auction stand."

Lola searched the crowd. "You're right. I don't see Detective Briggs. This doesn't really seem like his thing. I don't think I've ever seen him take part in the auction."

"Wish you'd mentioned that before I put the thing together. Would have saved me a great deal of humiliation. Then to have Mayor Price standing there begging some poor sap to offer a buck or two—ugh. I should just head home right now."

"Why would you do that?" Mom asked.

Lola and I turned back. My parents had finished their stroll on the beach. Dad's cheeks were so red from the wind it looked as if he'd dipped into Mom's blush.

"She doesn't want to suffer the embarrassment of no one bidding on her basket," Lola said airily. She was smiling about her proclamation until she caught my expression. Her mouth straightened into a grim line. "Guess I should have kept that nugget closer to the chest, eh?"

"Yep."

Dad pulled out his wallet. "Nothing to worry about, kiddo. I've got three dollars and I'm going to place the whole wad down on the first bid."

"I'm going to go down to the sand and bury my head," I muttered from the side of my mouth so only Lola could hear. She was too busy fighting off a laugh to pay attention.

Her eyes widened and she stood up straighter. "There's my basket. It used to have a bunch of balls of yarn in it, so hopefully the sandwich isn't going to have tufts of wool all over it."

"Ryder would still eat it like it was lobster and steak." I looked Ryder's direction. The second Mayor Price read the name on the basket, he stood up tall and at attention. He quickly scanned and easily found Lola in the crowd. A few seconds later, he was plopping down a whopping forty bucks for the basket. A generous bid that earned a round of applause from the crowd.

"Oh jeez," Lola muttered. "I wish I'd slapped together a better sandwich." She headed toward the stand to pick up her basket.

"Well, at least you garnished it with wool," I called, now feeling some revenge for her blurting my humiliating predicament to my parents. Dad was standing anxiously by with his three dollars, but he seemed to be rethinking the whole thing after hearing Ryder's bid.

"You know, Stan," Mom said. "I made that sandwich. You could at least break out the debit card. I'm sure they'll take it."

"What for? I get your sandwiches for free at home. And I don't have to eat them in the sand."

I turned to him and kissed his cheek. "Dad, I love you but if you bid on my basket at any amount, I will climb under the covers of my bed and not come out again until New Year's."

Reluctantly, he jammed the wallet back into his pocket. "I understand, kiddo."

Seconds later, Mayor Price said my name through the megaphone. I was certain I heard a sneer in his tone, but it was hard to hear over my pounding heartbeat. I turned to my parents. "Why don't we head home. I'm done here tonight."

"What do I hear for the first bid?" I could hear the mocking in Mayor Price's tone.

"But, dear, let's at least wait to see how much your basket fetches," Mom said.

"No one is going to bid on it, Mom."

"Twenty dollars," a voice came through the crowd. I didn't need to follow the sound of it. It was Dash.

Mom pinched my elbow hard enough for me to squeak in protest. "It's that handsome neighbor of yours." She seemed to think she was whispering, but it bordered more on a loud mumble.

"Yes, Mom, I recognize him." I was stunned to hear Dash bid on it, especially after I'd turned down his date offer. I couldn't find Kate in the crowd, so I passed it off as Dash being hungry and Kate not showing up with a basket.

"Thirty dollars," the next bid came through the crowd from another familiar voice, one that sent a slight tremble to my knees.

Mom practically jumped into the air to get a look at the second bidder. Detective Briggs had left his coat behind, a smart move in the summer heat. The sleeves of his white dress shirt were rolled up and the collar was open. The casual, yet official, attire looked exceptionally good on him. Neither man looked my direction. Their focus was on the basket.

"Forty," Dash called over the heads of the spectators. His offer sent a mild, curious rumble through the group.

"Fifty," Briggs yelled.

Mom squeezed my arm again. She finally spotted the second bidder as he stepped closer to the stand in his stark white shirt. "Is that—?"

"Yes, that's Detective Briggs." My pulse was racing and splattering in every direction. The auction was not turning out quite the way I'd predicted. Mayor Price's mouth looked like he'd been sucking on a lemon. He seemed reluctant to ask for the next bid. But that didn't stop Dash.

"Sixty dollars," Dash called.

A much louder mumble rolled through the crowd. I wondered just how many rumors were going to be started from this one public event.

"Maybe they know I made the sandwich," Mom suggested.

"Thanks for the vote of confidence," I whispered back.

Dad moved forward to stand next to me and watch more closely. "It's not your sandwich, Peggy. It's my little girl. Everyone wants to spend time with her. Can't blame them."

I leaned over and kissed him on the cheek. I was feeling extra nervous and giddy, like I was back in high school. It was nice having my always level-headed dad nearby.

"A hundred dollars!" Briggs' offer caused a collective gasp in the crowd that was loud enough to send the three persistent seagulls waiting around to see if one of the baskets was for them into the sky.

I'd been keeping my head low but I knew a lot of attention was being shot my way. I snuck a surreptitious peek Dash's direction. His face had dropped along with his shoulders. He walked away dejectedly. I wasn't sure how to feel except I knew which man I wanted to win the basket.

"Sold to Detective Briggs for a hundred dollars," Mayor Price said with far less enthusiasm than it required.

"I'm glad I stuck one of Elsie's brownies in the basket," Mom said.

Dad's eyes widened with surprise.

"Yes, it's all been smoothed over," I muttered to him. "I'll tell you later."

"Miss Pinkerton, come pick up your basket." Price always said my name with a twinge of distaste.

A glaring silence fell over the crowd and every face turned my direction.

"Oh my," Mom chirped and waved. "Hello, everyone. Beautiful town, by the way."

"Peg, they are looking at Lacey, not you," Dad grumbled under his breath.

Everyone parted like the Red Sea as I walked toward the stand. Curious, amused gazes, some familiar, some unfamiliar, followed me. It felt a little like walking through the gauntlet.

"Hello," I said here and there. "Happy Birthday America, am I right?" I added.

I made a point of smiling at Mayor Price. He glowered back at me. His usual response. I grabbed the basket and found Briggs. He was wearing that slightly lopsided smile. My heart melted and a herd of butterflies kicked up in my stomach. The man just bid a hundred dollars for a sandwich and a brownie. Maybe there was more to our relationship than I realized. Then a slap of reality struck me. Or the wild bidding war might just have had to do with the personal war going on between the two men.

CHAPTER 12

$\mathcal{B}$riggs and I hardly spoke as we headed toward the grassy knoll in front of the lighthouse. I finally broke the silence.

"Hope you won't be too disappointed."

He looked at me in question.

"With the picnic basket, I mean."

"I won't be. I'm paying more for the company than the food."

I dropped my face to hide the blush warming my cheeks. It was rare when he talked like that. It was even rarer for me to blush at something.

We sat down on the grass, and Briggs placed the basket down in front of us. The sun was close to setting behind the horizon and the dusky pink sky hovering over the ocean made for a lovely picnic backdrop.

"How is work?" I asked. "Busy?"

"Actually, it's been kind of dull. Not too much going on. It's good news but it makes the work day slow." Briggs leaned back on his hands. His tanned forearms flexed below the rolled up shirt sleeves.

"Well, I wouldn't worry about that for too long. I can smell trouble in the air."

Briggs squinted one eye as he grinned at me. "I knew that nose could smell a speck of cinnamon a mile away, but I didn't realize it could smell trouble."

I shrugged. "Maybe that's more my intuition than my nose. It just seems things have been a little too quiet. Don't you think?"

"The old calm before the storm theory?" And just as he said it, the air filled with a thunderous sound like the beating of forty whale hearts. There were sputters and coughs in between an explosive rattling sound that sent every bird and ground squirrel in the vicinity running for cover. I jumped to my feet in alarm, but Briggs reached into the basket for his overpriced sandwich.

"That's Burt Bower. He goes out fishing every night in July and returns at exactly 7:30. You can set a watch by it. His boat should be laid to rest at the bottom of the sea, but he keeps bringing it back to life every summer."

The scent of burning oil drifted toward us. I covered my nose and mouth. I blinked my eyes to keep them from watering.

Across the pier and marina, I could hear loud complaints being tossed toward the boat owner. Eventually, the rambunctious engine shut off. It felt like someone hit the mute button. Thankfully, the pungent smell was carried off by the wind. I was about to suggest that Burt ask Dash to check out the engine but quickly remembered who I was talking to.

Briggs pulled out the sandwich. Mom took pride in her sandwich building skills, and the turkey and cheese in his hand was a piece of art. "Wow, I guess I wasn't expecting such a great looking sandwich." He recognized his mistake instantly. "I mean—not that you aren't perfectly capable of—it's just that it—"

I rapped his shoulder with the back of my hand. "Stop while you're ahead. Besides, I didn't make it. My mom did. Not that I wasn't willing to put time and my thoughtful touch on the meal, but when my mom saw me pulling the ingredients out of the bag, she swooped in and took over. It's sort of her thing—taking over. I'm just waiting for her to remake all my flower arrangements more to her standards."

Briggs gave me half the sandwich. "I saw your parents standing with you during the auction. When do I get to meet them?"

Preferably never was what I wanted to say. "Anytime you want. They are just meandering around the town and cruising up and down the coast in the convertible my dad rented."

Briggs swallowed a bite of sandwich and nodded. "Delicious. So your dad is the convertible type, eh?"

"Only in his daydreams."

We were sitting one short hill climb away from the garden club booth. Carla was sitting on the stool in the booth looking lonely and miffed. It seemed Vernon was still enjoying his fried chicken with Jenny.

Briggs motioned toward the booth. "How is the new club going?" he asked with the same amused tone that Elsie used when she asked about the club.

"As a matter of fact, it's just fine. I donated all those herbs to sell at the festival." He picked up the snip in my tone.

"Sorry, I didn't mean to tease." He leaned closer. I picked up the faint scent of his soap. It seemed he'd switched brands. I liked it. "Why does Carla look so upset?"

"Apparently, Jenny Ripley makes her fried chicken the way Vernon's mom used to make it. So every year, ignoring his wife's dismay, he goes out of his way to buy Jenny's basket."

The story gave Briggs a good laugh. "You've got to admire a guy who sticks to his guns about fried chicken." He reached into the basket and pulled out the bottle of iced tea Mom had tucked inside. Briggs leaned closer and took a deep whiff. "I smell something chocolatey."

"Fudge brownies," I declared happily. "Of course, if I'd had the time, I would have labored over a hot stove to make them for you myself, but Elsie brought in a tray. Guess I don't need to say more than that."

"No, no you don't. I love Elsie's fudge brownies. By the way, I don't think brownies are made on the stove."

I elbowed him lightly and laughed. Right from our first meeting, James Briggs and I had been comfortable with each other. He had been reluctant, and rightly so, to let a complete amateur sleuth like me anywhere near his official investigations. But once he realized what an asset my nose was on murder cases, he acquiesced and allowed me to help. Now he even invited me to join in on investigations. Something that delighted me to no end.

Briggs' Adam's apple held my attention while he tilted the tea bottle and finished it. He had a nice manly throat. (Yes, it was a strange thing to focus on but it was the truth.) He lowered the empty bottle with a 'that hit the spot' sigh. "How is the Hawksworth murder investigation going?"

"To tell you the truth, I haven't had much time to work on it since I snuck in and opened that old trunk in the gardener's shed."

Briggs turned to me with a raised brow. "I should warn you that you are talking to an officer of the law and anything you say might be used against you. Especially if it includes breaking and entering. Something I've caught you doing on more than one occasion."

I placed my hand against my chest. "Me? Breaking and entering? I don't need to break anything. Surely you've heard of Garth, the infamous lock destroyer? Apparently, his handiwork is still in use all over the town. Including the shed."

"Yes, I know about the broken locks and Garth. I wasn't always a cop, you know? I even had fun occasionally and did scurrilous things like sneak into the gardener's shed with—" He stopped. "Never mind."

"Oh wow, that's quite the cliffhanger you just left there, Detective. But you're right. Back to the original subject. Lola showed me how old trunks and jewelry boxes had hidden key compartments. So I snuck, I mean, walked into the shed one night and found the key compartment on the old trunk. My investigation got stopped because someone had followed me to the site. Your murderous ex-art teacher, to be exact." I shuddered involuntarily at the thought of a killer stalking me around the dark house site. I shook the tremor from my body and took a deep breath. "The Hawksworth museum the town is so proud of is hardly worth a dime when it comes to evidence about the murder, but there were a few things inside that trunk that looked promising. My parents want to walk up there tonight. I might use Garth's lock system to poke around in the shed."

"Just be careful when you're up there poking around."

"I will be but at least this time there won't be any psycho art teachers lurking around in the shadows."

CHAPTER 13

I should have known better. The auction and picnic and, in general, the day had gone way too smoothly. I was feeling too at ease about everything. That was always the case when something unexpected and unpleasant happened—when I was feeling too pleased with my life.

Briggs carried the empty basket as we strolled back toward the flower shop. I spent a good portion of the walk trying to decide whether the night would end in our first kiss. It seemed like the perfect ending to the picnic. And frankly, it felt as if we'd just finished a date, so a kiss would be the natural conclusion.

Briggs looked ahead to the sidewalk in front of the shop. "Where's your car?" he asked.

"I rode my bicycle to work."

He stopped in front of Franki's Diner. "What? It's too dark to ride your bike. We can get my car."

"There are plenty of streetlights along the way and it's such a short trip. Really, I'll be fine." Before we could start off again, I took hold of his arm. "But thank you for worrying."

Franki's neon sign reflected off his brown eyes as his gaze held mine. He moved his arm to hold my hand. "Lacey," he said quietly. He always called me Miss Pinkerton when we were doing investigative work, but when we were enjoying each other's company for social reasons, he switched to Lacey. I liked the way it sounded.

I stared up into his eyes, making sure to give every indication that I was waiting for that kiss. Heck, not just waiting but expecting, anticipating, about to jump out of my sandals ready for it.

"Yes . . . James." I rarely called him James, but I liked the way it sounded too.

He leaned a few inches toward me. A gentle breeze blew between us. I closed my eyes and parted my lips.

"Olivia?"

I kept my eyes closed. "No, it's Lacey, but that's all right. Mistake forgiven." I waited but his hand dropped away.

I opened my eyes as he skirted around me and walked toward a woman coming out of the diner. Not just any woman but the undeniably pretty woman with glowing skin and auburn hair Lola and I had seen at the Corner Market.

"James." The woman stopped and blinked her large, almond shaped eyes at the man who had been just seconds away from kissing me. I was beyond deflated. I was devastated.

The woman, Olivia apparently, took a moment out of her shock at seeing *James* to check out the woman he had nearly kissed. Briggs finally seemed to recall that I was standing behind him, just recuperating from a missing kiss.

"Olivia, this is—uh, Miss Pinkerton. Miss Pinkerton, this is Olivia."

I couldn't speak. The wind was sucked out of me when he called me by the formal name. Obviously, he didn't want the beautiful Olivia to know we were out socially and on a first name basis, no less.

Olivia reached out to shake my hand and added an interesting detail to the introduction. "James and I used to be married."

Since the wind had already been taken out of me, all I could do was nod and force an awkward smile.

I could feel Briggs' gaze on the side of my face. I worked hard not to make eye contact. It was the last thing I needed at the moment. I finally had enough breath in me to speak. "Nice meeting you. I was just on my way home. Good night, Detective Briggs," I said sharply and still without looking at him.

I headed down the sidewalk. My shoulders tightened as I heard his footsteps behind me. "Lacey, wait. Just give me a second and I can drive you home." He reached for my hand, but I pulled it quickly away.

I stopped and faced him with my best stony expression. I didn't want him to see how upset I was and I most definitely didn't want his lovely ex-wife to see. "Thank you for the offer but I'd much rather ride home. Good night, Detective Briggs." He visibly flinched at the harsh way I said his name. Job well done. I didn't want to leave behind even a splinter of ambiguity about how badly the night had just ended.

I walked fast and then ran toward the shop. I was thankful that I had my bicycle and not my car. I needed to work off some emotion and cool my head before I got home to Mom's million questions about the picnic.

I unlocked my bicycle and rolled it out to the sidewalk. A light was on in Lola's shop. For a brief second, I considered walking over to tell her just how disastrously my night had ended but then I saw Ryder's head in her front window. It seemed her night had gone much better than mine. Maybe a bicycle ride and home to my bed was my best bet. After all, my pillows and quilts never disappointed me. Tomorrow was a holiday. Maybe I could stay in my wonderful bed all darn day. That thought brought me to the fireworks show and the *date*. It seemed that was a farfetched notion after all.

CHAPTER 14

*N*evermore nudged me awake with his head. I rubbed his ears and turned around on the bed, drawing the covers up over my face. After the terrible end to the evening, I rode my bicycle home. It felt as if I was dragging a cart of bricks behind me the whole way, but I knew it was just a giant lump of disappointment. Along the way, I rehearsed what I would tell my parents about the nice picnic and good food and slow sunset on the horizon. They didn't need to know more than the basics. I was sure that would satisfy Dad, if he cared at all. But I worried Mom would drill me about Briggs and our friendship. I didn't want to talk about it. As luck would have it, after the long mental preparation for the scene at home, I walked inside and found they had gone to bed early. The entire house, even pets, was fast asleep. I was relieved and headed straight into my own room.

"Lacey," Mom's voice sang down the hallway. "Sweetie, I'm making my traditional red, white and blue pancakes," she called. "Up and at 'em."

On any other day, Mom's patriotic pancakes, fluffy buttermilk cakes topped with powdered sugar, strawberry glaze and fresh blueberries would have sent me down the hallway like a torpedo. But the last thing I wanted this morning was food. All I needed was my quilt for cocooning and my pillows for muffling sounds and smells. I buried my face into my pillow and wrapped the blanket around me. Of course I knew that Mom wasn't going to give up with just one holler down the hall. And I was right.

Seconds later, she yanked the quilt from my head. "Hurry before your father eats them all. Oh, and Dad let the bird out. He's standing on the kitchen counter staring at the box of Fruit Loops. Should I pour him a bowl?"

I tossed my covers aside. It was too warm for a quilt cocoon anyhow. Apparently bed sulking was best done in the cold months. "No, he doesn't want the cereal. He has a crush on the bird on the box."

Mom stopped in the doorway and looked back at me with a wide-eyed blink. "Did you just say your crow has a crush on the cereal box?"

"Not the box. The Fruit Loops toucan on the front of the box. I guess he's got beak envy or something. Mom, don't be offended, but I'm not really in the mood for pancakes. Just a cup of coffee, please."

"Not hungry for pancakes." She wiped her hands on her apron and came to sit next to me.

"Mom, you're not going to—"

She reached over and placed her hand on my forehead to check for a temperature.

"O.K. I guess you are. I'm not six anymore, Mom. I know when I've got a fever. I'm just not hungry."

"Oh dear, did something happen last night?"

I quickly searched my mind for the monologue I practiced all the way home. It had vanished. "Last night was fine. I'm just not a big breakfast eater anymore." I got up from the bed to show her I was fine and fever-free. "I need to ride down to the shop."

"But I thought the shop was closed today for the holiday."

I grabbed some shorts from my drawer. "Best day to catch up on dull paperwork." I had no intention of sitting down to paperwork. I doubted I'd be able to concentrate on any numbers or orders. What I really needed was to ride my bike, get some fresh air and hopefully run into Lola. She was the only shop owner who'd decided to have a quick morning sidewalk sale on the holiday.

Dad showed up in the doorway holding a plate and eating a pancake.

"Stanley, take that back to the table before you drop blueberry and powdered sugar everywhere."

"You act like I'm walking around the house waving my pancakes at the end of the fork. Everything is going straight from the plate to my mouth." Dad looked at me. "Kingston wants Fruit Loops."

"No, he has a crush on the toucan," Mom said matter-of-factly, as if it was a perfectly normal thing.

I waited for Dad to start a line of questioning or break into one of his famous belly laughs. He just shrugged and shoveled another forkful into his mouth. He carried his plate back to the kitchen. I went into the bathroom to get showered and dressed.

Mom and Dad were still at the table picking at the remaining pancakes and sipping coffee. Kingston had returned to his perch. The cereal box was back in the cupboard.

"I thought it was better to separate him from the toucan," Mom whispered.

"Why are you whispering?" Dad asked. "It's not like the crow can understand you."

I poured myself a cup of coffee. "I wouldn't be too sure about that, Dad. Anyhow, I'll just be gone for an hour or so. If you'd like, we can walk up to Hawksworth Manor when I get back."

Mom sat up straight. "Yes, let's do that. It looks so spooky and gothic from your backyard. I'd love to see it up close."

I drank the coffee and put the cup in the sink. "Great. I'll be back in an hour." I headed straight out to the garage and wheeled my bike to the driveway. I didn't even look in the direction of Dash's house. I didn't want to see him . . . or Briggs . . . or anyone, except Lola.

I climbed on and rode downhill toward town. The morning air cooled my face and helped revive me. I knew once I cleared my head, the night and the lost kiss would fade away. I wasn't one to waste time fretting or stewing over feeling jilted.

Since most of the shops were closed, the town was close to deserted. People were probably using the day off to sleep late so they'd be rested for the night's festivities. I had no idea what was going on with Briggs and me. We hadn't talked and I hadn't heard from him. It certainly didn't feel like we were still going to attend the celebration together. I wasn't too sure I wanted to go at all, for that matter. I could see the show from my front yard and avoid all the chaos and crowds down at the beach.

Lola had stuck to her plan. She'd rolled a few pieces of mid-century furniture out to the sidewalk. Slick tables and chairs from the middle of the twentieth century were the new hot item in antiques. Unfortunately for Lola, her shop was stuffed to the gills with mid nineteenth century relics, as she called them, and those items were getting harder sell. Recently, she'd managed to snag some more modern pieces and had a hard time keeping them in the store. She'd placed a few sleek night stands and coffee tables out on the sidewalk, along with a shiny cherry dining table. I'd warned her that there wouldn't be many people browsing or walking Harbor Lane on the holiday, but it seemed she had a few people already checking out the furniture.

My shoulders sank and my legs slowed on the pedals. Lola would be too busy to talk. Still, I rolled on, deciding I could just hang out in the store and wait for her to have some free time. In truth, I was almost more anxious to ask her how her evening went with Ryder than to recount the terrible details of my night. As I rode past the Harbor Lane Medical Group my gaze flashed across the street to Kate Yardley's Mod Frock. There was a closed sign on her door, but I saw her standing in the front window glaring intensely at Lola's shop. Maybe she was angry because we'd all collectively decided not to be open for business—all except Lola, that is. Kate could have done the same if she felt so strongly about it.

One of the customers in front of Lola's shop turned to look at a pair of lamps. I pulled the brakes and my bike slowed and skidded to a stop. Lola's early morning customer was none other than the lovely Olivia or ex-Mrs. Briggs as she'd so plainly stated the night before. The whole event rolled back to me, the near kiss and the abrupt metaphorical cold splash of water at the end. I didn't want to see the woman with her flawless skin and golden glow. My therapy session with Lola would have to wait. I turned the bike around and pedaled hard and fast back home. Maybe what I needed was a trip to Hawksworth Manor for my ongoing murder investigation to take my mind off of James Briggs.

CHAPTER 15

$\mathcal{I}$t was a holiday. I had the day off and just twenty-four hours earlier I was thrilled with the prospect of sitting down to a spectacular fireworks display with Briggs. Now I was seriously considering hibernating in bed for the rest of the day. Only I had two energetic travelers staying in my house.

I pushed my bicycle into the garage and walked inside.

"You're back already?" Mom asked.

Dad was on the couch watching television and Mom was wiping down the kitchen counter. I was momentarily transported back in time and I was a kid coming in from a bike ride with friends. The house was my beloved childhood home instead of my cute little house on Loveland Terrace. Of course, Kingston was out of place. Back then he would have been standing on the front fence with the other crows instead of on top of his cage.

Mom pulled on oven mitts and scurried to the oven. "I kept some pancakes and berries warm for you." She emerged with a short stack of perfectly shaped pancakes. Butter dripped along the outer edges. A bright mound of berries sat on top.

Mom's brow dropped in a frown. "Or are you still not hungry?"

The few seconds of nostalgia as I walked in the door helped wipe away some of my glum mood. "Actually, Mom, pancakes sound good. Then we can walk up Maple Hill to the Hawksworth site. I'll fill you in on all the details behind its gruesome history."

"Did someone say gruesome?" Dad was adjusting his pale green shorts beneath his belly.

"Stanley," Mom said. "You and that morbid curiosity. You should see the weird stuff he watches on the science channel. He loves gore. The man who used to read you Goodnight Moon and P.J. Funnybunny likes blood and guts."

I swallowed the mouthwatering bite of pancake. "I forgot all about P.J. I used to love it when you put on that big goofy voice to narrate his parts."

"Do you mean like this, kiddo?" Dad hadn't lost his talent for voiceovers.

"Yes, that's it." I laughed. I finally caught my breath and took another bite. "Hmm, these are so good, Mom." I looked at both my parents and smiled. "I'm really glad you guys came." My throat tightened unexpectedly. I had to blink back tears. I realized how lucky I was to have such wonderful parents. Especially at a time like this when I was feeling down.

Mom brought me a glass of milk as I finished the breakfast. It was nice to be a kid again for those few minutes.

"Well, get your walking shoes on, parental unit. I'm taking you uphill to the pride and joy of Port Danby, the infamous site of a hundred-year-old murder."

It was a beautiful day, which went counter to our murder adventure, but we strolled cheerily along Myrtle Place.

I walked between my parents to fill them in on the story. "A wealthy businessman named Bertram Hawksworth built the estate in the late nineteenth century. He and his wife, Jill, had three children. Bertram was quite the entrepreneur, apparently. He had plans to build a shipyard down on the coast. Those plans were thwarted by Mayor Price."

Dad laughed. "I'm going to assume that's not the same Mayor Price as the one I saw at the picnic auction."

"No, but they are relatives. Harvard Price, mayor at the turn of the last century and three of his descendants, including Harlan Price, the current mayor, have been holding the mayor's office for over a hundred years. Anyhow, on to the murder. One dreary night, (actually I had no idea about the weather but thought it added to the atmosphere) the entire Hawksworth family, even the three children, were shot dead. The murder weapon was found in Bertram's right hand. It was immediately concluded that, in a fit of rage, possibly over losing the shipyard deal, Bertram killed his entire family and then killed himself."

"How tragic," Mom said and then quickly added that the Crape Myrtle Trees along the road gave the whole street a fairy tale quality.

"So it sounds like the case was solved," Dad noted. "Why is it a big mystery?"

"The police at that time closed the case without much investigation. But here's where it gets good and it lets me know that I'm a pretty good sleuth. I saw a picture of the murder scene. It was quite gory even though the quality of the hundred-year-old photograph was poor. But one thing was very clear. Bertram Hawksworth was holding the murder weapon in his right hand." As we reached the bend where Myrtle Place became Maple Hill, a car filled with noisy teenagers streaked past. I hoped it meant they'd cleared out for the morning. "As you can imagine, the place is sort of a hangout for kids. Anyhow, I went to the library in Chesterton. They have a wonderful room filled with old newspapers from the town. After a little research, I found a picture of Bertram Hawksworth signing the original contract for the shipyard . . . with his left hand."

Dad connected the dots quickly. Maybe I'd inherited my Sher-lock genes from him. "He would have been holding the gun in his left hand," Dad said.

"Yep, pretty elementary stuff. The original officer on the case made note of it on his report, saying he thought there should be further investigation. A week later, records show that he was hastily taken off the case and transferred to another precinct."

"Interesting," Dad said. "So someone walked into the house and shot the family and then planted the weapon in the father's hand to make him the culprit."

"Precisely," I said. "Only they didn't do their homework and they left behind a very large hole. So I've appointed myself the task of finding out who killed the Hawksworth family. I've found a few interesting tidbits here and there, some connected to Mayor Harvard Price, but nothing significant yet. I just don't have enough spare time to research it. But I've got time this morning. There's an old trunk I want to go through to look for clues."

"Wonderful. We get to tour the inside of the house?" Mom asked.

"No, it's chained off for public safety reasons. Although, I have been inside."

Dad chuckled. "Of course you have."

"It was a mistake. It's just a bunch of crumbling rooms and stairs. Definitely no longer up to code. I got stuck inside when the front door knob fell off as I tried to leave. It was a foggy morning and it got pitch dark inside. And you know how I feel about the dark."

Mom fell short of an eye roll. She was always convinced my fear of the dark was exaggerated. But I knew it was very real. "Lacey, I don't understand where on earth you developed that terrible fear of the dark."

Dad looked over at me. His face was getting pink from the sun and the hike. "Must have been all those times I locked you in dark closets," he joked.

I laughed and took hold of his arm. "Dark or not, I was never afraid when you were around, Dad. You were always my gallant, brave knight."

He kissed the top of my head. "And you were always my tomboy princess."

"The mush is getting thick around here," Mom quipped. She occasionally got jealous if I was lavishing too much praise and affection on Dad. "I've kept every nightlight you used in a box with some other keepsakes. We went through at least twenty."

"Thanks, Mom. Be sure to bring up that embarrassing anecdote when we're with my friends. And yes, that is sarcasm," I added quickly in case she took the suggestion seriously. "Anyhow, we can walk around the grounds. And we can look inside the original gardener's shed. There are a few artifacts stored inside. Just prepare to be slightly disappointed by the display. It's rather meager and unremarkable. It's worth a browse though. It'll give me time to look through the old trunk."

I was feeling better by the minute. Getting my mind off unhappy events was easier when I had a good mystery to solve.

CHAPTER 16

*M*y parents looked tiny and out of place standing in front of the multi-story manor with its pointy turrets, gabled roofs and broken windows. The manor was slowly being eaten away by time and harsh coastal weather. Soon, the six foot chain link fence surrounding it would be the only thing left standing on the site.

Mom pulled out her phone to take a picture. "It look like it's right out of a gothic novel. I'm half-expecting the ghost of Heathcliff to come floating out from one of those upstairs windows."

"Now that would be interesting," Dad said.

Mom leaned her head my direction. "He's been watching all of those silly ghost hunting shows. You know, the ones where they walk around in the dark and you can't tell what the heck is going on and then someone gasps dramatically and says 'did you hear that?' And I'm sitting on the couch next to your dad saying 'nope, didn't hear a thing but I'm getting good and seasick watching that camera lens dart from here to there."

Dad nodded. "Yep, that's exactly what she says. Every time. But she still sits down to watch it with me." He winked. "Where's this gardener's shed?"

"Right this way, folks," I said in my best tour guide impersonation.

I led my parents to the gardener's shed.

"I guess you weren't kidding when you said it was a shed." Mom circled around the side to look at the small building.

"Yes, no pretense on this tour, Miss." I pulled on the lock and it popped open.

Dad was peering over my shoulder. "It seems your mom was right about all that spinach she fed you considering you can break open locks with just a tug."

"Yes, well, that's a long story. Suffice it to say, the security system around this place is a bit lax. You coming, Mom?"

"Wouldn't miss it."

I propped the door open with a stone to allow in some natural light. Mom and Dad went right to the shelves to look at the old toys, dolls and leftover items from the home. I went straight to the trunk. It was still tucked under the shelf. It had most likely not been moved since I opened it. I knelt down on the dusty floor and reached beneath for the secret key compartment. The key clinkered to the floor. I pulled the trunk forward far enough to open the lid. The same century old dust hit me as I turned the key and opened the trunk.

I turned my head to sneeze.

"Bless you," Mom said. "You were right, dear. I've seen more interesting items in Lola's antique shop. I think I'll go and explore the grounds some more. This shed is too dingy and dark."

"I'll go with you and make sure you don't fall in any giant gopher holes," Dad quipped.

"Very chivalrous of you, Stan."

"Well, if we lost you to a gopher hole, who would cook breakfast tomorrow?" Dad said as they walked out into the sunlight.

With the shed to myself, I quickly pushed past the stack of decaying straw boaters and ascots and pulled out the leather bound account books. Following the money was the favorite mantra of any good investigator. I was certain the murder had something to do with the cancelled shipyard. There were two sets of account books. One set was dated 1885 to 1900. The next set was 1900 to 1906. That would take me to the year that Bertram Hawksworth died. I paged through the yellowed parchment. It was just columns of intricately handwritten numbers. People back then didn't have keyboards. Everything was done by hand, and they had much better writing as a result. The accountant, a Harold Moore, signed his name at the bottom of each page. Since I wasn't a book-keeper, most of the columns meant nothing to me. It seemed as if Hawksworth had a lot of income but he also had a lot of money going out. Typical for a big, important businessman, I assumed.

I thumbed through the book and noticed that in 1901 the handwriting changed to a lighter, more feminine looking script. I moved my eyes to the bottom of the page. Jane Price. I continued on. Jane Price, Mayor Harvard Price's daughter from a first marriage, had been Port Danby's treasurer for a short amount of time before leaving town. There didn't seem to be much informa-tion about why she left. It seemed, aside from being town trea-surer, she was also an accountant for local businessmen, including Bertram Hawksworth.

I flipped through some more pages and found different writing in 1902. The new accountant's signature was impossible to deci-pher, but it was not Jane Price. I got up on my knees to put the ledgers back inside and noticed a ribbon tied stack of letters on the bottom of the trunk. There were three letters all written in frilly script, a woman's handwriting. Each envelope was addressed to Bertram. No surname at all, just Bertram. Maybe the letters were written by Jill Hawksworth, the murdered wife.

The wax seals had all been broken, so I decided it wouldn't be too terrible to sneak a look at one of them. I pulled the crisp, folded parchment from of the envelope. Something dropped out. I reached down and picked up a brittle, dried flower. I could tell by the shape that at one time, apparently a hundred years ago, it had been a sprig of lavender. The air tight trunk and surrounding parchment had preserved it.

I moved the paper more toward the light to read the hand-written letter. It was dated April 1902.

Dearest Teddy,

A sprig of lavender from my garden. Let the fragrance remind you of that warm afternoon we spent on the hillside. Your words are still my poetry. I could spend my entire day writing letters to you, telling you about the dreams I have. All of them with you at the center. My heart aches for you, Teddy.

Forever yours, Button.

A shadow fell over the room. I squinted up from the letter into the sunlight. "Your mom says the bugs are biting her, and I'm ready for lunch. How about you, kiddo?"

"I'm still stuffed from pancakes, but I don't want Mom to suffer bug bites." I tucked the letter back into the ribbon and returned the letters to the trunk. "Let's head back down. I'll just be a second. I need to lock this up."

"Sounds good." Dad shuffled through the grit covered pathway to look for Mom.

I locked the trunk. My phone buzzed as I pushed the chest back under the shelf. I swept the floor with my foot to erase any tracks left behind. I pulled my phone out of my pocket. It was a text from Briggs. My chest felt heavy as I swept my thumb across to open the text.

"I'm sorry, Lacey, but I've got a lot of work on my desk. I'll have to skip the fireworks show."

Deciding my response wasn't even worth the effort of fighting the keyboard and autocorrect, I texted back the thumbs up icon.

He sent a second text. "Can we talk later?"

This time the response didn't take much thought. "Nope."

I put my phone back in my pocket. The time up on the hill had lightened my mood, but his texts sank it again. I wasn't terribly surprised that he cancelled. My intuition had told me it was only a matter of time.

CHAPTER 17

*I*f my parents hadn't been in town, I would have just skipped the fireworks show. But I'd been playing it cool so I could avoid any conversations with my mom about my cancelled date. I told her Detective Briggs had to work, a perfectly suitable excuse for someone in his line of business. Unfortunately, I couldn't come up with a perfectly suitable excuse for me to miss the celebration so I tagged along with them.

Mom packed some sandwiches and I lent them a large blanket to sit on. We left well before dark so my mom could find 'just the right' spot. As Dad pointed out, the fireworks would be up in the sky, so just about any place would be the right spot.

Dad parked his convertible along the town square. I noticed Briggs' work car was still sitting in front of the station. I tried to convince myself that maybe he did have to work. Only I wasn't buying it. It seemed I wasn't the best convincer.

We climbed out of the car. Dad took a good twenty minutes trying to get the convertible top latched, while Mom lectured over his shoulder, letting him know what he was doing wrong. We were almost directly across from the garden club booth so I decided to head over and let Jenny know I could help out if she needed. It wasn't as if I had a date or anything.

Even though Jenny and Molly had both decided not to wear the matching hats to the celebration, they were both wearing their respective, one of a kind hats. And it seemed they were none too happy about the other person's betrayal of trust. They were both standing in the club booth, red faced and talking animatedly. I couldn't hear what they were saying, but it was clear as day they were having a heated argument. It was hard to believe they'd be having such a turbulent fight about the hats. It seemed there was something else behind it. Jenny pointed to something behind her. Molly threw up her hands in response.

My eyes swept across the lawn toward the center of activity and in the direction Jenny had pointed. A large brightly painted sign said 'Port Danby Pie Contest'. The pie contest. I'd nearly forgotten what Elsie had told me about Molly possibly cheating and Jenny confronting her about it. It seemed like a strange time and place to accuse someone of cheating, but it was highly probable that the pie contest was at the center of their argument.

I contemplated walking up to the booth just to stop the dispute, but I wasn't much in the peacekeeping mood. It was only a pie contest. I was sure they'd get past their squabble quickly.

I headed down to the beach where almost everyone was gathering to stake out their viewing spots. The last remnants of sunlight were being doused by the night sky. In an hour or so, explosive, brilliant fireworks would light up the sky and the ocean below, creating the perfect backdrop for a romantic evening. And I'd be sitting with Stanley and Peggy Pinkerton.

I scanned the crowd and spotted Lola's red hair. Ryder was holding a large blanket and searching around for the best spot. Just like I'd spotted her through the crowd, Lola found me too. Good friend that she was, she knew from the look on my face that something was up. She said something to Ryder. He glanced my way, waved and then started spreading out their blanket. Lola made her way to me.

She took hold of my hands and started in before I could utter a word. "I've got to tell you something. That pretty lady we saw in Corner Market—"

I nodded before she could finish. "I know. She's Detective Briggs' ex-wife. I've named her Olivia the X."

Lola's shoulders deflated, not so much from me spoiling her surprise ending but because she was a good friend. She could see I was upset. Lola crinkled her nose. "Did you meet her or something? Or worse? Did you see them together?"

"Worse."

A group of teens stomped between us, kicking up sand dust and laughing as they looked around for a place to sit. Lola motioned with her head. "Let's walk down by the water. It's too noisy up here."

"No, Lola, I don't want to take you from your date. Go be with Ryder. I'll be fine. Just a little hitch in my life that will smooth out soon."

"Right." She lifted her finger and drew an invisible air circle around my face. "But that's not what I'm seeing here. You listen to me whine and complain about men all the time. Let me be the sounding board for once."

"If you're sure."

"Yes. It'll help boost my self-esteem if I know I'm not the only one with guy problems."

"Oh well, in that case, it seems I'll be doing you a favor." I laughed as we headed toward the water. Dozens of boats had floated in and anchored in the waters off Pickford Beach to watch the display. Music, laughter and loud voices were rumbling from every direction.

Lola and I slipped off our sandals to walk on the wet sand.

Cold, frothy water lapped at our bare feet. Even though it was close to dark, a group of industrious kids were still working diligently on a massive sand castle.

"Briggs and I had a nice picnic."

"I left the auction but the rumors about the bidding war between Dash and Briggs were a hot topic for the rest of the night. Is it true Briggs paid a hundred bucks?"

"Yes, I was stunned to say the least."

"That just shows how much he likes you."

I kicked at the water around my feet. "Or it shows how much he dislikes Dash."

Lola stopped and looked at me. "Give yourself some credit, friend."

In the distance, over her shoulder, I could see, smell and hear Burt Bower's fishing boat rumbling into the marina. A tail of smoke followed the rusty vessel as it waddled and gurgled toward shore.

Lola looked back toward the water. "That man and his noise machine. Every summer we have to put up with that ridiculous fishing boat." She faced me again. "What happened after the picnic?"

"Briggs offered to walk me back to the flower shop. We stopped in Franki's parking lot." My face warmed as I thought about that moment. "It seemed we were about to kiss. Then boom, Olivia the X, Briggs' beautiful ex-wife sashayed out of the shadows. Well, not the shadows so much as the neon lights above the diner. By the way, in case you're wondering, she was just as lovely under harsh neon lights."

"I wouldn't worry about it," Lola started but was immediately interrupted by the deafening clamor of Burt's boat as he maneuvered it into the marina. A simultaneous round of hisses and boos shot up from the beach. Some were even waving their fists at the smoky boat as it sputtered to shore with all the delicacy and subtlety of a herd of raging, snorting bulls.

There was no use for Lola to continue. Even though she was right in front of me, she would have had to shout for me to hear her. The pungent smell of burning oil made my eyes water. I covered my nose to shield it from the onslaught of odor. I motioned with my head for us to go back up to the sand.

We headed away from the water. Ryder was sitting on the blanket, looking anxious to get the evening started. I hugged Lola. "I'll let you get to your date," I said loudly in her ear. "I've got to find my parents. Have fun."

After ten minutes of noise and smell, Burt got his boat moored. I scanned the crowd for two wayward looking parents but didn't see them. But I did find one other interesting scene as I surveyed the spectators. Dash was leaned against a light pole on the pier, casually engaged in conversation with none other than Olivia the X. It looked as if they knew each other, but I could have been reading the whole scene wrong. It seemed I'd been reading a lot of things wrong lately.

CHAPTER 18

Glowing red sparks frittered across the black sky. The display ended with a sonic boom style sound that echoed off the coastline. Pickford Lighthouse, one of my favorite parts of the town, looked stately and serious with the glittering patriotic backdrop.

I leaned closer to my dad. "I wonder if our humble little lighthouse feels like Lady Liberty on these nights."

Dad chortled. "I'll bet it does. You know, I'm sorry that you had to sit with us tonight instead of that nice detective."

I leaned over and kissed his cheek. "I'm not. I wouldn't change a thing about tonight, Dad."

Another round of fireworks shot into the sky, lighting the beach up like daylight. Mom covered her ears to block out the sound. In between bursts of color, she managed to get in snippets of conversation.

Mom looked over at me. "How come Elsie and Lester didn't come out to watch the display?"

"Elsie told me the noise was too much. She prefers to watch it from her house," I said.

"Lester is on call for the fire department." Dad was happy to impart that detail.

Mom leaned forward to look at Dad. "I forgot Les was a retired fireman. Well, that's nice of him. Are you still going fishing tomorrow morning?" she asked.

"Sure am. As long as he doesn't get called to any big fires tonight." It was obvious that Dad was excited about his fishing trip with Les. They were well suited to each other. I had no doubt they'd get along like cereal and milk. Mom and Elsie's planned baking event, on the other hand, had me less confident.

"Are you baking with Elsie tomorrow?" I asked.

"Yes, in the evening. After she's done with her work day." Mom shook her head. "That woman has the energy of a hummingbird."

I picked up my bottle of iced tea. "Yep, I'm thirty years younger and she can run circles around me. Literally. I've tried to run with her occasionally, but I always end up feeling like an out of shape slug next to her."

Mom clicked her tongue. "Nonsense. You look wonderful. Dad and I were just saying that." She leaned forward again. "Isn't that right, Stan?" Dad was already focused on the next light display, which seemed to be building to the finale. Mom huffed at his inattention and sat back. "We were both saying how wonderful and happy you looked. Except last night, after the picnic." She put up her hands. "But you don't have to tell me a thing. Just know that we are proud of what you've done here, and any man would be lucky to have you."

"Not sure how the two things are connected but thanks, Mom." I had to talk very loudly to be heard over the thunderous booms above. A quick succession of big explosions in gold, silver, blue and red covered the sky like glitter tossed on a black floor. Even the stars above looked impressed. I leaned closer to Mom and raised my voice over the clamor. "I am happy in Port Danby. It's a quiet, peaceful town," I said loudly just as the noise above ended. The rest of the beach was quiet, the onlookers awestruck by the finale, so my voice carried across the sand.

The silence in our quiet, peaceful town was suddenly broken by a woman's scream. A murmur vibrated across the sand as people looked around to find the source of the sound. "Help!" a woman yelled from across the grassy knoll in front of the lighthouse. "Call the police. I think she's dead."

The murmurs erupted into gasps and alarmed voices as people hopped to their feet. "Stay here," I said as I pushed to my feet. "I'll go see what's happening." A small crowd started to gather under the tree and around the garden club booth. A siren pierced the air, but the sharp sound was dulled by the low thump in my ears left-over from the fireworks. It seemed as much as I wanted to avoid Detective Briggs this evening, I was about to run smack into him.

"Excuse me," I said and made my way between the press of bodies gathering around the garden booth. "Please let me through." I could smell my basil and rosemary pots as I squeezed my way up to the front. But it wasn't just herbs and the leftover smell of fireworks penetrating my nose. It was the metallic scent of blood.

I elbowed my way to the table and looked over the boxes of herbs. Jenny Ripley was lying face down on the grass, her back covered in blood. It didn't take an expert or my short stint in medical school to know she was dead.

96

CHAPTER 19

I was completely annoyed that the mere sound of his voice sent a lone butterfly fluttering around my stomach. Especially considering the grisly scene in front of me. Doubly so because I knew the victim. I'd only just become acquainted with Jenny Ripley when I joined the garden club, but I couldn't understand why anyone would want to kill her. She was a sweet, energetic, smart woman.

"Officer Chinmoor, please get these people back at least thirty feet. Folks, make room for the paramedics." Detective Briggs sounded more stiff than usual.

I finally willed myself to look back toward the sound of his voice. Our gazes latched on to each other's briefly before splitting apart. I could almost hear a snap as the line of sight between us broke.

"Folks, you've got to move back. You are impeding the first responders from doing their jobs." Officer Chinmoor, the young officer who was second in charge at the Port Danby Police Station, was always far less patient and far more dramatic with his orders at a crime scene. He was about to scoop me up in the crowd as he urged everyone back until Briggs spoke up.

"Miss Pinkerton can stay."

I had mixed feelings about it. I was thrilled to be included in the murder investigation, but at the same time, I felt taken for granted. What if I didn't want to be included at the crime scene? I wasn't on payroll, after all. I nearly laughed at that thought. Who was I kidding? Of course I wanted in on the investigation. And poor Jenny Ripley. She was just selling a few herbs for the garden club funds and she ended up dead. Shot in the back, from what I could see. Her sparkly hat, the one that had caused a stir, sat next to her head as if it had been pushed off in her fall.

Two paramedics circled behind the front of the booth and crouched down next to the victim. I already knew what their assessment would be. And so did Briggs. But it was always better to put on a hopeful show for the surrounding onlookers. It was less shocking.

Backup police from the neighboring town pulled up with lights spinning. I scanned the crowd and saw Molly's face, looking pale and stunned. Carla and Vernon were standing farther back in the group. It seemed it wouldn't be long before the entire town knew that Jenny Ripley was dead. Briggs turned to Chinmoor. He was doing an admirable job getting the anxious townsfolk back.

"Chinmoor, now that backup is here, let's clear the entire area. Also, find the person who discovered the body. I need to ask her some questions."

The paramedic, a young man who looked fresh out of medic school, looked up at Briggs and shook his head.

"It's a gun shot," I said.

Briggs was standing right next to me, but he didn't look my way as he answered. "It would appear so." He pulled out his phone. "Nate Blankenship is on call tonight at the coroner's office." After

the awkwardness of the night before, we had been thrown uncere-
moniously together by an unexpected murder.

"Lacey? Lacey," Mom's worried tone rose from the crowd. She
pushed Officer Chinmoor's arm out of the way and marched
across the lawn toward the murder scene.

Before I could tell her to go back, Briggs spoke up sharply.
"Ma'am, we need you to stay back and away from the scene."

Mom's mouth dropped in dismay at his tone.

I rushed toward her. "Mom, you've got to stay back with the
others." I walked her back to where Dad was standing.

"Sorry, kiddo, I tried to hold her back, but when she saw you
standing there with the paramedics, she broke free." Dad took
Mom's hand. "Peggy, let Lacey do her work."

"Thanks, Dad."

"Don't do anything dangerous," Mom called as I headed back to
the scene. Behind me I could hear Dad.

"How can it be dangerous, Peggy? She is literally surrounded by
police officers and paramedics. If she was going to face down
danger, this would be the perfect time for it."

I bit my lip to avoid smiling at Dad's comment. It was most
definitely not a time for a smile.

Briggs met me as I headed back to the scene. "I'm sorry, I didn't
see that it was your mom."

"No, you were right to send her back," I said coldly and firmly.
"Do you need me to do my nasal inspection?" I sounded so busi-
ness-like, I hardly recognized my own voice.

Briggs paused. It seemed he was thrown off by my distant tone.
"Uh, yes, if you don't mind."

"Very well." I headed confidently to the body. Lights had been
brought in, and they highlighted Jenny's hands. Just a few days ago,
I'd taken a tray from those hands, hands that spent hours embroi-
dering pillows and labeling an extremely organized house.

"Miss Pinkerton?" Briggs' voice came through the moment of sadness. "Are you all right?"

I cleared the lump from my throat. "Yes, sorry. I'm fine."

"You knew the victim, didn't you?" he asked. I was trying to ignore the empathy in his deep, smooth voice. It only added to the vast, confused mix of feelings I had about the man.

I cleared my throat a second time. "We recently became friends when I joined her garden club."

"Yes, I knew you were part of that." He pointed to the box of herbs. "Are these yours?"

"Yes, they were my contribution to the booth. That way I didn't have to spend time sitting behind this table. Of course, at the time, I had plans for the firework show." I looked plainly at him.

"I'm sorry." He reached up and smoothed his longish hair back. It did that little curl up the collar thing it always did when it got just a bit too long.

"Sorry for what?" I said flippantly. "I had a wonderful time regardless. At least until this." I circled the counter and entered the booth. The rhinestones on the patriotic cap sparkled like diamonds under the police lighting. Several of the silver stud stars were on the edge of the back table where Jenny lay. A few more had broken off and landed in the grass next to the hat. I ran my nose close to Jenny. Gory wounds didn't usually affect me. Medical school had hardened me to blood and death but tonight was different. I closed my eyes as I neared the bullet hole in the back of Jenny's dress. The overwhelming scent of blood masked every-thing else. I could hardly even pick up the scent of grass beneath her.

I moved to her hands, deciding if there was anything of note it would be on her fingers. The heady mix of herbs pummeled me but there was a hint of something else in between the earthy aroma of basil and rosemary. I stopped and sat up to take a breath of air and clear my sinuses. I leaned down again and breathed in. Separating out the smells in my mind, I came up with the mystery smell. Cinnamon. It was faint but it was a smell that was easy to discern no matter how many odors swirled around it.

Briggs politely offered me his hand to help me to my feet. I used the edge of the table instead. His disappointment was palpable.

"Blood, grass, smoke from overhead, herbs." I pointed out the pots unnecessarily. "And a touch of cinnamon." It almost sounded as if I was reciting a recipe.

Briggs had out his notebook but there wasn't much to write. Every scent was expected with the exception of cinnamon.

"Cinnamon?" He double checked before writing it down. He tapped his pen on his chin. "Wasn't Jenny the judge in the pie contest?"

"I believe so." My answers were curt and brief. Just wasn't in the mood for cumbersome dialogue or the usual banter tonight. But his question reminded me of the argument I had witnessed between Jenny and Molly.

I looked past him to the crowd that had been moved farther back. I couldn't find Molly amongst them. Many of the onlookers had left the scene. It had been a long night of festivities, which ended rather abruptly with an ugly murder. It seemed most didn't need to see any more of the tragic scene. I couldn't blame them. As much as I loved a mystery, this one left me feeling down. Jenny just didn't seem like the type of person someone would hate enough to kill.

Officer Chinmoor was escorting a woman across the grass. She looked hesitant about getting too close to the garden club booth. Which made sense, of course. She was a sixty something woman who I'd seen working at the pharmacy. Her skin color matched her gray hair and she gripped Chinmoor's arm for support.

"Detective Briggs," Officer Chinmoor called from a good

twenty feet away. "Mrs. Terrence doesn't want to get any closer. She's the woman who discovered the victim."

I followed along with Briggs. He didn't tell me to stay behind, but something told me, this evening I could do anything and he wouldn't dare say no. Besides, we'd gotten fairly comfortable in our routine. He was even willing to refer to me as his assistant on certain occasions.

"Mrs. Terrence," Briggs wrote her name as he spoke. "Thank you for returning. I know this is difficult and I'm sure you want to go home and rest, but if you could just tell me what happened tonight."

Mrs. Terrence's blue eyes landed on me. I nodded politely. She took a shuddering breath. "The fireworks show was about to end— I could tell because it was getting extra loud. It always gets terribly loud at the end."

Briggs stopped writing and prodded her to continue with his Detective's smile, a subdued, somber version of the real thing.

"Anyhow, I thought I would swing by the garden club booth to get some basil and rosemary. I knew that they'd be shutting down as soon as the festival ended, so I hurried over just as the fireworks were ending. The garden club booth was over here, away from everything else. As I walked toward it, I was disappointed. I didn't see anyone so I was sure they'd closed up. But I saw the herbs and I thought, well, I could leave some money and just take what I need-ed." She covered her mouth to stifle a sound that seemed half sob and half sigh of disbelief. "And as I picked up the pot of basil, I glanced down." Her voice wavered.

I reached across and patted her arm. It seemed to help calm her.

"There she was, laying there, not moving, with blood all over her dress." She sucked in a breath. "Poor Jenny. Poor, poor Jenny."

"Thank you, Mrs. Terrence." Briggs closed his notebook.

"Officer Chinmoor, please see that she gets home all right." Chinmoor led the shaken woman away.

"You know everyone in the club, right?" Briggs asked.

"Yes."

He walked back to the booth and picked up a piece of paper that had been tucked under the herbs. It was a schedule. "According to this schedule, Molly was supposed to be running the booth from seven until nine. Do you know if she's here tonight?"

"Yes, I think she is. And I don't know if this is relevant, but I saw Molly and Jenny arguing earlier in the evening. Might have had something to do with the pie contest."

"Great, then I guess I'll start with Molly."

CHAPTER 20

The coroner's van pulled up before Briggs could start any interviews. He gave Officer Chinmoor a list of some of the people he wanted to talk to before they left for the night. It was basically the garden club members, Molly Brookhauser, Carla Stapleton and Virginia Kent. He already knew I was sticking around so he didn't add me to the list.

While Nate Blankenship examined the body, I searched out my parents. They were sitting on the pier watching the boats in the marina. A breeze had kicked up to agitate the water in the slips just enough to make the moored boats look as if they were part of a synchronized dance. It was helping to move the smoky haze from the air. Mom had draped the sitting blanket around her shoulders. She hunched down into its warmth.

Dad saw me first. "There you are, Lacey. We need to get Mom home. It's getting cold out here on the water and she has a headache."

Mom popped her face free of the blanket. "It's not a terrible headache, just a dull ache from all that noise."

"Noise," I repeated. Obviously Jenny was shot during the fireworks show. That was why no one heard it. I tucked that revelation away. "Mom, there's some aspirin in the medicine cabinet. Why don't you take a warm bath when you get home."

Both of them looked surprised. "Aren't you coming with us?" Dad asked.

"I'll probably stick around and help Detective Briggs for awhile longer."

Mom gave an angry shake to rid herself of the heavy blanket. From the lift of her chin, I sensed I was about to hear her ardent opinion about something. And I was fairly certain of the topic.

"I don't know why you help that man with anything. First, he breaks off your plans for the fireworks show. Then he was extremely rude to your own mother. That neighbor of yours, Dash, now he is a gentleman. If you ask my opinion—"

"Which she did not—" Dad muttered.

Mom ignored his comment. "I think you are focusing your efforts too much on the wrong man."

That was my mom, she could sandwich unwanted advice between even less wanted opinion, then top the whole thing off with a zinger. And all with a headache.

"Mom, I'm not focusing my efforts on anything but my own life."

"Good girl," Dad cheered quietly. He knew he was going to hear about his interjections later but that didn't stop him.

"And this has nothing to do with my neighbor or the detective. Who, by the way, would have spoken that way to anyone who thought she had the right to break through the police line and barge onto a murder scene."

"There was no line," Mom insisted with another chin lift.

"It's implied. When you see a crowd of people jammed together and no one's toes are going past a certain point, that's a police line. And I'm staying because I like to help out on investigations. I'm good at it and it gives me a chance to use my hyperosmia for something other than smelling Elsie's baked goods through the shop wall. Besides, Jenny, the dead woman, was a friend of mine. I want to help find her killer."

Dad stood up and offered Mom his hand. She basically slapped her palm down on his. Yep, he was going to get an earful tonight.

He winked at me. "You go curly haired Sherlock. I'll get Mom home and to that bath. She'll feel better in the morning."

Mom got up. Her chin was still high in the air. "I feel just fine. But I don't think we should leave our little girl out here alone on this cold beach with murderers stalking about the place."

Dad swept his arm toward the street. "Again, Peggy, she's surrounded by law enforcement people. I think she'll be fine. Let's go before you work yourself into a migraine. Or until you pass that headache on to me."

I saw my parents off and headed back across the lawn to the murder scene. Officer Chinmoor was just finishing up his favorite duty of enclosing the scene with yellow caution tape as I reached the booth. My little pots of herbs looked wilted and sad in the midst of it all. It was hard to believe just hours earlier the location was a garden club fundraising booth and now it was the focal point in a homicide. While we occasionally came across a scene where it wasn't immediately known if it was murder or an accidental death, it was crystal clear this time. Jenny's ruthless killer had seemingly shot her in the back.

The coroner was briefing Briggs. His assistants were moving Jenny's body onto the gurney. I took a closer look at her face. There was a long, thin gash on her forehead and grass on her mouth. Her hat had already been picked up and placed in an evidence bag along with the single pot of thyme she had apparently been holding when she fell. My herb pot was going to be sitting in the evidence room along with the festive hat. The team was still searching for the weapon.

Briggs approached me with some caution, as if I might turn around and snap at him or run off like a rabbit from a fox. His brown eyes landed on my face. There was a second of emotion there which I quickly shut down with my stony all-business face.

"I have a theory about the time of death," I said.

"Actually, Nate has already put the time of death somewhere between seven and nine tonight. I checked with the pyrotechnic people. They said the show started at 8:45 and ended at 9:15. Since the place was crowded and no one heard a gunshot, we can only assume Ms. Ripley was killed during the show." He had put on his dry, detective tone, and I was regretting my coldness. Then I reminded myself he deserved it. "What was your theory?"

My shoulders deflated. "Exactly that. A gunshot would have been easily camouflaged by the loud firework display."

Briggs looked around and then down at his notepad. It seemed he preferred to look anywhere but at me. "No weapon yet. But since we can assume the murder happened during the show, it'll be easier to narrow down alibis. We need to find out where people were during the show. You mentioned you smelled cinnamon on the victim. If you don't mind, I'd like to have you come along for the interviews just to see if you can pick up the similar scent."

"I don't mind at all, Detective Briggs," I said primly.

He flinched at my tone, then turned to me. "Lacey, we should talk."

"In the middle of an investigation? Hardly. We'd better hurry, people are heading home. We might miss our opportunity." I could feel his gaze on my back as I walked purposefully toward the pier.

CHAPTER 21

$\mathcal{M}$y brush off of a *talk* with Briggs seemed to have put him in a tense mood, rare for him. Most of the time he managed to stay cool and smooth as cream, no matter what the situation. Apparently, having the lovely Olivia the X in town was making him uptight.

I spotted Molly's sparkly hat in the distance and picked up my pace.

"Miss Pinkerton, wait for me." I was used to him referring to me as Miss Pinkerton when we were investigating a murder but somehow, tonight, it just sounded wrong. It might have been the edge of tension in his voice. He caught up to me.

"Is that Molly in the hat?" he asked as we both kept picking up speed as if we were in some kind of walking race.

"Yes, it is. Kate Yardley sold both Jenny and Molly the same hat. She also told each of them the hats were one of a kind." I normally wouldn't have added that. It seemed I was mad and I was taking it out on Kate. Not that she didn't deserve it this round.

Molly was standing in front of the salt water taffy stand

helping the woman behind the booth return taffy to the appropriate containers. It might have been my imagination or it might have been the lighting on the pier, but it seemed Molly's face paled when she saw us. She knew we were coming to talk to her.

Molly tossed a bowl of strawberry taffy into the container and turned to greet us with a mournful sigh. "I just can't believe it, Lacey," she spoke directly to me and hugged me. I was sure it was on purpose to let Briggs know she saw no reason to talk to the police. As she pulled away, I smelled something sweet, like vanilla. There might have been a touch of cinnamon in there too, but it was mostly an artificially sweet vanilla scent. It could have been from taffy.

"Ms. Brookhauser," Briggs began, "if you don't mind, I'd' like to ask you a few questions."

Molly looked properly shocked and perplexed as she glanced at the woman behind the taffy stand. The other woman was short with hair that matched the color of the lemonade flavored taffy. I'd seen her several times in town and was fairly certain her name was Rachel.

"I can't imagine how I could be of any help," Molly said after her small act had ended. "But ask away."

Briggs pulled out his notebook and got his pen ready.

"Poor Jenny," Molly said with a shake of her head. "She worked all those years and was finally enjoying her retirement and then bang. Dead with one shot."

Briggs' gaze caught mine. We might have hit a rough spot socially, but we were still in tune during the investigation. Molly was hardly acting like the truly devastated friend. And she knew that Jenny had been shot once.

"May I ask how you knew Ms. Ripley was shot once?" Briggs took the words right out of my mouth.

Molly wasted no time with her answer. "Why, everyone knows. Jodie Terrence has been retelling the horrible moment when she found Jenny all over the marina. She said there was a hole in Jenny's back. What else could that be except a gunshot? I guess there was too much noise tonight for anyone to hear. Poor, poor Jenny. You should talk to that neighbor of hers, Percy Troy. They had a big dust up about that darn wall and the property line. Percy was madder than a rabid raccoon about having to build the wall and lose three feet of property to boot."

It never made you look less guilty if you immediately started dropping names and possible suspects. I knew Briggs was thinking the same thing. I wondered who thought of it first though. Not that it was a competition. He was, after all, the professional, and I was just a talented snoop and sniffer. But I liked to think I was becoming more in tune with my sleuth side every day.

"Ms. Brookhauser," Briggs continued after jotting down a few notes. I always loved watching him with his rather last century tools of the trade, paper and pen. But tonight, it was hard to think he looked adorable with his notepad. I was still too upset. "Where were you during the fireworks show?" he asked.

Molly looked right back at her taffy friend. "Why, I was right here the entire show. Rachel and I watched the display from the taffy stand. She can vouch for me."

"Full name please," Briggs requested from Rachel.

"Rachel Holder, you know me, Detective Briggs. My nephew, Louie, played football with you in high school."

Briggs nodded. "Yes, Louie Holder. How's he doing?" It was unusual for Briggs to get sidetracked during an interview but everything about him seemed off tonight.

"He's great. He is an optometrist in Wisconsin. Has three kids."

Briggs nearly dropped his pen when she said three kids. "Wow, three. Well, good for him. Mrs. Holder, can you verify that Molly was with you during the entire fireworks show?"

Rachel nodded. "Yes, I can. We both sat right here and watched the whole thing from the taffy booth."

"Did either of you leave the booth at any point during the show?"

Rachel shook her head. "Nope. We were here the whole time."

"Thank you. Oh, one more thing, Mrs. Holder. How are you and Molly acquainted?"

"We used to work together at Parson's Grocery Store in Mayfield," Molly piped up.

Briggs looked at Rachel for confirmation. "Yep. She was in deli and I was in produce. We've stayed good friends for years."

Briggs wrote a few things down. Molly glanced my direction and suddenly seemed put off by my presence. "Lacey, I've heard you often work alongside Detective Briggs. Interesting to see it for myself." There was just enough insinuation in her tone to make me stiffen.

I forced a grin. "Yes, thank you. By the way, why weren't you at the garden club booth during the show? I noticed you were on the schedule. You left Jenny there all night." I didn't know Molly well, but the few interactions I'd had or witnessed left me thinking we'd never be friends.

"I know. I felt bad about that. But Rachel needed help. Taffy is a much more popular product than herbs." Her mouth pursed as if my herbs were somehow humorous.

"Thank you." Briggs stepped in to stop the slightly heated exchange. "I might need to ask you more questions later."

I forced a polite nod and we walked away.

"One thing is certain—" Briggs said. "Molly is not terribly upset over the loss of her friend."

"You noticed that too?"

CHAPTER 22

*D*etective Briggs and I asked around and were told that Carla Stapleton and her husband, Vernon, were at the pie contest table helping clean up. I quickly filled Briggs in on the few things I knew about Carla on our way to the pie table.

"I've only recently become acquainted with Carla. She is a member of the garden club. At the last meeting, Molly was extremely unpleasant to Carla, rolling her eyes about her slow reading of the minutes. Carla has bad eyesight. Molly also let everyone know that Carla had replanted nursery bought dahlias in her garden instead of growing them from tubers. But Jenny came immediately to Carla's defense. I can't imagine why Carla would kill her, even if Vernon prefers Jenny's picnic basket to Carla's."

"That's right. You mentioned the fried chicken problem when we were eating our picnic." Both of us fell silent for a moment.

"Lacey," he said quietly.

"Not now, Detective Briggs. They are packing up the pies, and I just remembered I want to taste a few of the samples." I hurried ahead. "Carla, hold on."

Vernon stepped out from behind Carla as I reached the table. "Oh, hello, Vernon, I didn't see you there." I wanted to erase my comment immediately.

"I'm sure you heard, Lacey," Carla said. "The pie contest was cancelled. Of course." She pulled a tissue out from her pocket and blew her nose. It was red from crying. She was visibly shaken. "I still can't believe it."

"It is terrible," I said and then quickly picked up a sample of pie. Everyone at the table, Briggs included, raised brows at me.

"Oh, I'm sorry. It's just I tend to get very hungry when I'm upset." I shot a secret wink at Briggs to let him know I was looking for something specific. Namely, did Molly actually enter a bakery pie?

The pies were labeled with letters. I picked up the slice of apple pie because I knew it would contain cinnamon. Fortunately, Carla supplied me with the baker's name. "That one is Molly's. Mine is the lemon. Frankly, I'm not disappointed that the contest was cancelled because Molly's pie wins every year."

Vernon stepped forward. I knew Briggs was confused by the size difference. They were quite the odd pair standing side by side but then what law ever stated that the husband had to be bigger in stature than the wife.

"Dear, I've told you again and again not to even enter the contest. All it does is upset you," Vernon said. He rolled his eyes toward Briggs in a 'women, am I right' sort of way. Briggs smartly did not show reaction.

Briggs held up his notebook. "Mrs. Stapleton, where were you during the fireworks show?"

Carla seemed perplexed by the question. "Down on Pickford Beach with the rest of the town watching the show of course."

"Did you sit with anyone in particular? Someone who could verify that you were there?"

Vernon lifted his shoulders to make his chest bigger. "Not sure what this is about or what you're implying, Detective Briggs," he said sharply.

The cool, calm Briggs had snuck back in when I wasn't looking. "I need to verify her whereabouts during the murder."

"Like some sort of alibi?" Carla asked with wide nostrils.

"Yes, if that's what you want to call it," Briggs countered smoothly.

Vernon took hold of Carla's hand. His wife's hand was much larger. "Carla was sitting with me through the entire show."

Briggs wrote down a few things, which seemed to irritate the couple. Carla's height put her at an advantage. She stretched her neck up to see what he was writing, but Briggs was skilled at keeping his notebook out of view.

I took the opportunity to taste Molly's apple pie. Flaky crust stuffed full with tender, sweet apple slices. And plenty of cinnamon. I lifted the next forkful closer to my nose before taking the bite. Vanilla was less obvious than the cinnamon but that made sense. The pie was dotted with plump currants that gave an extra kick at the end of the bite. With as many pies as I'd eaten in my life, I wasn't skilled enough to tell whether it was home baked or from a bakery. What I did know for certain—it was not one of Elsie's pies. Cheating was one thing but being brazen enough to enter one of Elsie's pies in the contest would be a whole other level of impudence.

"Is there anyone else who could verify that you were sitting on the beach for the fireworks show?" Briggs asked. "Other than your husband, I mean."

Carla nostrils were still spread wide with exasperation. "Yes, as a matter of fact two people can verify my story. My neighbors Tom and Sarah Hopper. Now, if that's all, I need to get this cleaned up."

"Yes, thank you. Oh, one quick question though. When did you last see Jenny Ripley?"

Carla crossed her arms and glowered down at Vernon.

"I ate the picnic dinner with her yesterday," Vernon volunteered easily. "It was delicious too. We talked about this and that, her retirement, the problem with her neighbor, Percy Troy." Vernon's eye rounded. "That's who you should talk to. Percy Troy."

"Yes, I've made a note of that. Is he around?" Briggs asked.

"I don't think I've ever seen Percy show up for the Fourth of July festivities," Carla said. "He's somewhat of a recluse. Of course, he might still have been here sometime this evening," she said pointedly.

The conversation had ended, but I was working on figuring out all the ingredients in the pie by smell. I took another bite and looked up to find all eyes on me. Including a certain detective's amused brown ones.

"Sorry. " I put the remainder of the pie in the trash can. "Like I said, I get hungry when I'm upset." I eyed Carla's pie. "Do you happen to use cinnamon in your pie, Carla?"

She laughed. She'd been upset about the murder but not terribly upset, it seemed. "Cinnamon in lemon pie?" She laughed again.

"I suppose that would be strange."

"Thank you for your time," Briggs said. He flipped his notebook closed and we walked away.

"Did the pie tell you anything or were you really just hungry?" he asked.

"Maybe a little of both. Molly's pie does have cinnamon, the scent I picked up on Jenny's hands. I know the contest was a source of contention between Molly and Carla. I also know that Jenny was planning to confront Molly about the possibility that she was cheating by entering a bakery pie."

Briggs looked over at me. "Elsie's apple pie?"

"Please, no one would be that silly. There are bakery pies and then there are Elsie's pies. They are a whole different species of pie."

"Good point." We reached Officer Chinmoor. He had just finished combing the area for evidence.

"Any luck with that weapon?" Briggs asked.

Chinmoor smiled. "No weapon but we found the bullet shell." He held up the baggie.

Briggs took it in his hand and examined it with the light from his phone. "Never seen a shell like this. We'll get forensics to work on it. In the meantime, make sure the site is cleared of spectators for the night."

I caught a yawn before it rolled from my mouth. "If you don't need me anymore, I think I'll head home."

Briggs looked around. "How are you getting home? Do you need a ride?"

"Nope. I just saw Lola and Ryder walking across to the Town Square. They'll drop me at home."

Briggs momentarily broke eye contact to hide his disappointment. He lifted his face again. "Thank you for your help, Miss Pinkerton."

"Anytime, Detective Briggs." I was certain I could feel his gaze on me as I walked away. At least I hoped he was still looking.

CHAPTER 23

*D*ad was up early eating the egg sandwich my mom prepared for him. He was as excited as a kid waiting to go to an amusement park. Something told me going fishing with Les would be the highlight of his vacation.

Nevermore curled around my feet as I poured food into his bowl. Dad looked over his sandwich at me. "That bird wants to fly around today."

I laughed. "Did he tell you that?"

"Nope. I can just tell. He's antsy."

I glanced across the room to Kingston's cage. He was nibbling on the peanut in his dish, looking anything but antsy. But Dad was right. He needed to get out.

"I've got to go outside and check air quality. Make sure there's not too much smoke."

Mom walked out from the guest bedroom and set her bottle of sun block on the table next to Dad's arm. "Lather this on or else you'll get even more wrinkles."

Dad peered sideways at the bottle. "Now all I can smell is that darn sun block. This egg sandwich tastes funny now. And who says I don't want wrinkles? I think they make me look distinguished."

"No, they make you look like a prune," Mom quipped. "Lacey, what should we do today while your father is out fishing?"

I picked up a plate with eggs and toast. "I've got to go into work for a few hours. But I'm closing early, by lunch. We could head over to Mayfield. You said you wanted to do some shopping."

"Yes, that sounds good. Then I'll just stay here for the morning and read my book. It'll be nice and relaxing after last night with the noise and the murder and all."

Dad chuckled. "Not exactly your run of the mill Fourth of July celebration. I mean talk about ending with a bang."

"Stanley," Mom said sharply. "It's hardly a laughing matter."

Dad nodded. "Yes, sorry. Did they find the killer?"

I didn't sit to eat, which earned an eye roll from Mom. "Not quite that easy, Dad. The perpetrator doesn't usually step forward at the crime scene and say 'it was me'. Unfortunately, the few people we interviewed last night, women who I knew had a beef with Jenny, the dead woman, had solid alibis. We've concluded the murder happened during the thirty minute fireworks show because the noise masked the gunshot."

"Makes sense." Dad picked up his coffee. "Any other leads?"

"Not yet but they found the bullet shell. I'm sure that will produce something."

I rinsed my plate and finished my coffee. Kingston became animated when he saw me pick up my backpack. "That's right. Let me check the air." I walked out onto the front porch. The coastal breeze had pushed most of the lingering smoke inland. The sky was crystal blue with only a touch of the acrid taste of smoke in the air. I went back inside. "You're in luck, King. You can fly along with me as I bike to town."

Mom sat at the table with a plate of eggs. "So, you're off and

Dad is leaving and Kingston." She looked at Nevermore who had stretched himself out on the floor to lick his paws. "Guess it's just me and the cat."

I kissed her cheek. "Thanks for breakfast. I'll be back at noon. Dad, put on sun block and have fun."

I opened the garage to get my bicycle. Dash's truck was gone. He was probably already working down at the marina. After spotting him with Olivia the X, I hadn't seen him all night. I was sure he'd be at the show with Kate. Come to think of it, I hadn't seen Kate either.

I climbed on the bike. Kingston took off ahead of me. It had been a few days so he definitely needed to stretch his wings. I needed to stretch my wings or at least my legs some too. It was a beautiful morning so I decided to take the long, scenic route to the shop by heading down Culpepper Road past the farms and down to the lighthouse and beach before circling back to the shop. Naturally, I had an ulterior motive for the detour. I planned to ride down Maplewood Road where Jenny and Molly both lived. Jenny's house was at the end. Molly lived several doors away. It was easy enough to spot Molly's house with its impressive flower and vegetable garden. Her red sedan was in the driveway but the house was quiet.

Kingston spotted me pedaling down an unfamiliar street and swooped down to see what I was up to. The fact that the garbage cans were still out front due to the holiday probably had something to do with his interest too.

I rode up to Jenny's pretty farmhouse. Soon, the colorful blossoms and flourishing plants dotting the fence in the front yard would be drying up from neglect. From what I knew about Jenny, she'd lived alone in her Victorian farmhouse since her husband's death.

It was probable that Detective Briggs would eventually search the house for clues into her death, but at the moment, the place looked quiet and untouched. My investigative instinct told me to search around the house for an open window or door, a common occurrence in the small town of Port Danby. But I didn't want to risk having Briggs catch me inside before he had a chance to go through the place. We just weren't on solid enough footing at the moment. I was sure he'd be angry. At least far more annoyed than usual.

I heard a rustling noise down the street and saw that Kingston had set himself the task of drawing an empty box out of Molly's trash can. His big wings flapped as he pulled the box free. It fell on the road, which was Kingston's goal. He paced around the box, checking it out, trying to decide if it had been worth his effort.

I rode back toward him. "Kingston, this is what street crows do. Not crows who wake up with a handful of snacks in their personal feeding trough."

He ignored me and quickly grabbed what looked like pie crust out of the box. He carried it up to a tree where he could finish his stolen snack in peace. I picked up the box and saw that it was from Mayfield Bakery. Only crumbs were left in the box. I lowered my face to take a deep whiff. Apples and cinnamon. It was hard to know for certain without tasting the pie from the box, but it could easily have been the same pie I tasted at the contest table. That would mean Jenny had been right about Molly cheating. My eyes swept back to Jenny's house. Her trash can was sitting out front. It made me sad to think just yesterday she was rolling the bin down to the road and today she was dead.

On a whim, I decided to check Jenny's trash can. I had a farfetched notion that if Jenny knew about the pie, she might have bought one from the bakery for proof. The can was filled with lots of tidbits of embroidery yarn. Jenny must have been straightening up her embroidery supplies.

I wasn't planning to go too deep into another person's trash, but after pushing aside a few empty cartons and potato peels, I spotted the same bakery box. I held my breath to avoid breathing in the mix of odors coming from the can but managed to wrench the box free. It was wet from the potato peels but not much could mask the smell of cinnamon. It was one of those fragrances that could permeate a room with hardly any effort.

I put the box back into the can. It wasn't going to do much toward solving the murder but it solidified the idea that Jenny had very likely confronted Molly about cheating in the pie contest. Granted, it was a wildly ludicrous motive for killing someone, but at the moment, it was the only motive I could come up with. Jenny just didn't have many enemies.

I shielded my eyes with my hand to look out at the property behind Jenny's house. Percy was not out toiling on the wall. I was sure he'd already heard about his neighbor's death. I wondered if he took that as a cue that he could just skip the whole thing. From what I remembered, he was on the losing end of a legal fight where he ended up having to pay for the wall and lost three feet of property. Now *that* was a much stronger motive than pie.

I climbed on my bicycle. I'd given Ryder the day off, and I wanted to spend time with Mom. I would open the shop for a few hours and then drive her to Mayfield. And while we were there, we could stop in Mayfield Bakery for a slice of apple pie.

CHAPTER 24

"You're home already," Mom said. She set down her book and stretched her arms up. Nevermore had curled up next to her on the couch. "I thought you might stay longer."

I walked into the kitchen for a glass of ice water. "No, it's quiet in town. The after holiday lull. And that's what's brilliant about being my own boss. I can shut down the shop whenever I have a mom to entertain. By the way, Elsie said four o'clock at the bakery. She's looking forward to your baking session."

"I am too." Mom hopped up from the couch. "Where to? You mentioned a shop that had lots of kitchen and tableware. I'd love a new platter for my Thanksgiving table."

I nodded. "You and your holidays. The sparkler smoke hasn't even cleared away and you're thinking about your Thanksgiving table."

"Time goes fast when you're my age. By the time I get back home, they'll be setting up pumpkin patches around town. Well almost. Anyhow, I'm ready if you are."

I drained the ice water. "I am now. Let me just call in my wacky crow." I opened the door and whistled. Seconds later, Kingston waddled across the threshold with his beak forward and his *hands* behind his back.

Mom watched with amusement. "My goodness, he really does think he's human."

"Actually, I'm pretty sure he considers himself a step or two above our species." Tired from the flight around town, Kingston readily hopped into his cage and onto his favorite section of perch. I shut the cage.

"Let's go. I'm hungry for some pie."

"Pie?" Mom asked as we headed out the door. "You should have told me. I would have baked one. I'll make one tomorrow. What kind?"

We climbed into the car. "Actually, I need to check out the apple pie at Mayfield Bakery. It has to do with the murder."

Mom buckled her seat belt. I pulled out onto Loveland Terrace.

"How on earth does apple pie have a connection to the murder? Besides, I thought the woman was a gardener not a baker."

"Jenny was a retired librarian. She was talented in many things. You should see her embroidered pillows. Just your thing. She had a different one for each holiday."

"Some people are so talented. I tried to embroider once. Needless to say, I ended up with a lot of pricked fingertips, tangled embroidery thread, a collection of new curse words and nothing that resembled the cute little kitten picture I was going for. But you haven't explained how the pie is connected to her murder?"

I drove down Myrtle Place toward the turnoff to the neighboring town of Mayfield. "It's probably not. I'm just grasping at straws, or in this case, pie crust because I can't figure out why anyone would kill Jenny. She was the kind of woman who had too many friends and very few enemies. Jenny was the official judge of the Fourth of July pie contest. A woman named Molly had been winning every year with her apple pie. I think Jenny recently discovered that Molly had been buying her contest pie from the Mayfield Bakery. I'm fairly certain they argued about just that before the fireworks started."

"Hmm." Mom moved her chin side to side in thought. "Was there a big cash reward for the winner?"

"As far as I know, the only reward was a blue ribbon and the satisfaction of knowing you baked the best pie in town. Elsie's not allowed to enter, otherwise the ribbon would be hers and no one else would bother to enter."

Mom gazed out the window at the shops as we headed toward the center of town. "What a cute little commerce center. Wish we had something like this back home." She turned to me. "If there was no cash reward, it seems like a flimsy motive. Unless Molly didn't want her pie scam exposed because then people would know she was a cheater. But still, killing someone just to save face? Seems farfetched."

"I agree. I'm out of sorts with my whole investigation this time. I guess my head and heart just aren't in it."

Mom's brow arched. "*Your* investigation? Are you officially part of the team?"

I thought about her question. I certainly always felt like part of the team. Briggs always included me on new details in murder cases, but since our friendship was on tender ground right now, I didn't feel that connection. I felt almost like an outsider. That must have been why I didn't do my usual brazen snoop job by looking for a way into Jenny's house. I didn't feel like I had a right to search it. Which technically, I didn't. Though that'd never stopped me in the past.

The kitchen and tableware store was near the bakery. I found a parking spot in between, right in front of the coffee shop.

Mom unbuckled her seatbelt. "From what I've learned through

books and movies, motives usually have to do with money or crimes of passion. You said Jenny's picnic basket was the source of some marital tension. Maybe that's where you should be looking. Just my two cents though. What do I know?"

"A lot, actually. Now, why don't you start perusing that kitchen store. I'm just going to run in and buy a slice of pie to make sure Molly was definitely cheating. Even though it probably won't help solve the murder, at least I'll know what kind of character Molly has. She's not the kindest individual. Cheating in a pie contest would just add another layer to her personality. Not saying that you go straight from pie contest cheat to murderer but . . ." I stopped not sure how to finish because I knew it was a fragile connection at best. "It's all I've got."

Mom opened the door and grabbed her purse. "Well then, why don't you just let that brash detective figure it out all on his own. It's what he gets paid for." Even though he shelled out a hundred bucks for the sandwich she created, Mom was not letting go of Briggs first ditching me for the fireworks show and then speaking harshly to her at the murder site. I wasn't in the mood to defend Briggs at the moment either.

"I'll see you in the shop in just a minute, Mom. I'd ask if you wanted anything from the bakery but that would be silly since you are going to be baking with Elsie tonight."

"Yes, I am." She stopped. "I hope I don't seem like a clumsy amateur to Elsie."

"Mom, you're still my favorite baker in all the world. No, you won't seem clumsy or amateur. And Elsie will welcome your company."

That seemed to satisfy her. She headed down the sidewalk to the kitchen shop and I stepped into the bakery. I was in luck. There was one slice of apple pie left behind the glass.

The bakery clerk was young, a high school junior or senior. She still had a mouth full of braces but that didn't take away from her gracious smile.

I glanced at the goodies behind the glass and realized just how gorgeous Elsie's cookies and cupcakes were in comparison.

"What can I get you?" she asked.

"I'd like that last slice of apple pie, please. I'll eat it now."

"Sure." She picked up a plate and slid open the glass.

"Summer job at the bakery," I quipped. "What a treat."

She smiled politely at my corny joke. Oh my gosh, I was *that* age now where the teens humored me, all the while thinking poor, old woman and her old lady sense of humor.

She put the slice of pie on the plate and straightened. Her gaze landed on something behind me and stuck for a moment. I expected to turn and see the one thing that I was sure could hold her attention—a cute boy. I glanced back. Yep. Only it wasn't a cute boy. It was an exceptionally handsome man. My exceptionally handsome neighbor to be exact. My eyes drifted to the person next to him. Olivia the X. It seemed they were heading next door to the coffee shop. Port Danby had the Coffee Hutch, the best coffee shop in the area, but Dash and Olivia the X had made a trip to Mayfield to have coffee in the less superior shop.

Dash's bright green eyes swept into the bakery and landed directly on me before he yanked his gaze away and dropped his face.

"Ma'am, ma'am," the voice behind said several times. Yep, I was *that* age too. The ma'am age. I was still trying to sort out what I just saw as I pulled my money out and paid the girl.

I carried the pie piece to one of the small tables and sat down. I had no real appetite for apple pie or anything for that matter. I was sure I only needed a few bites. It was a decent pie. Cinnamon, tart apples, flaky crust and currants. It was the same pie that Molly had entered into the contest. There was no more doubt about that, but matching the pies had left me feeling fairly deflated. I didn't have much. I thought about Mom's comment on motive being money or a crime of passion. Maybe I was completely off track with the pie. Or maybe I was so bamboozled by what I'd just seen, my mind could no longer make sense of anything. If nothing else, it seemed I had another mystery on my hands.

CHAPTER 25

wo hours combing meticulously through the kitchen and tableware store ended with one brand new spatula. Mom held up the shiny silver pancake flipper and admired it in the sunlight coming through the windshield.

"This is the kind I've been looking for." She ran her finger along the front edge. "See this paper thin edge. Perfect for getting underneath a thin crepe without tearing it."

"Then I'm glad the shopping trip was a success." I didn't mention seeing Dash to Mom even though it might have been an opportunity to dull some of that shine she saw when she gazed up at Dash with those fuzzy, future son-in-law glasses. After I confirmed my pie suspicions, I walked quickly past the coffee shop, not wanting to be seen. Only it was sort of like walking past that proverbial car wreck where curiosity forces you to look. I snuck a quick peek inside the shop and saw that Dash was sitting across from Olivia. They weren't at the table in the window but farther in where it took a second to find him. Only then did I manage to spot him because Dash was taller than most people. The conversation looked about as casual as it could be between two impossibly good looking people. It was hard not to muse that they were quite a good match. But how on earth did they become a match at all? Just a few days earlier, Dash was asking me to the fireworks show. Was Olivia the X's visit unexpected? Or maybe they'd only just met. It would be crazy to think that Dash saw her walking on the marina or at the diner and immediately swooped in to do his Dashwood Vanhouten thing. But the big million dollar question was—did Dash know he was sipping lattes with Briggs' ex-wife? The plot might have been thin and threadbare around the murder, but it was definitely thickening around some of my men friends.

I was deep in thought when I turned onto Loveland Terrace.

Mom sat up straighter. "Oh look, it's your handsome neighbor."

I nearly hit the curb. Dash was walking out of his house with his dog, Captain, on a leash. We had spent a long time in the store so it made sense that he'd finished his coffee date. If that was what it was—a date? The coffee part was irrefutable.

"Hurry up," Mom said.

I lifted a brow at her. "Uh, all right hold on teen version of Mom. Settle it down. You taught me yourself—never look too anxious. It makes them think you're easy."

She swatted my thigh with her spatula. "See, I knew this spatula was special."

"Ouch." I rubbed my leg and pulled the car into the driveway.

"I just think you should talk to him. See how his day was."

I suppressed a grin because I had some insight into his day. But if I let even a flicker of a smile go, Mom would catch it and ask the meaning behind it. She was that good as far as reading her kid's facial expressions. (Which probably meant that I hadn't changed my expressions since I was a kid.)

As badly as Mom wanted me to talk to Dash, I wasn't in the mood to face him. I was certain he saw me standing in the bakery.

I purposefully rolled up the driveway at a snail's pace. Mom was just about to jump from the car while it was still rolling, so I finally put it in park.

She opened the door and waved her shiny new spatula. Dash was just to the far corner of my house. "You hoo, Dash, how are you?" Mom called.

I considered just crouch walking into the house in an attempt to not be seen, but I was sure Mom would yell out 'why are you walking like an old man, Lacey?'

Dash hesitated on the sidewalk and looked as eager to talk with us as I was to talk with him. But we had the social queen of the world between us waving her new pancake flipper like a scepter.

Dash put his free hand in his pocket and walked Captain toward us. With his broad shoulders bunched higher than usual and his hand in his pocket he looked like a guilty kid just coming home from school with a detention note to sign.

"Lacey took the afternoon off and drove me to the town of Mayfield. It's a nice little place. Not as nice as here, of course."

Dash nodded. "I agree." He finally found the courage to look my direction.

I found some courage too. "I could have sworn I saw you walking into the coffee shop."

Mom's face snapped my direction. "Really? Why didn't you say something? We could have stopped in for a latte."

"I think Dash was busy with a friend. I didn't want to intrude."

My comment stunned him for a second. "Uh, yes, I was having coffee with an old friend."

I'd found my courage. Now that I'd opened the gates, I decided to pry a little deeper. There had always been a mysterious source of anger between Dash and Briggs, and since I'd been caught in the center of it on more than one occasion, I felt I had every right to dig into their past friendship. His use of the word *old* triggered a few alarm bells. He certainly wasn't using it in the literal sense about beautiful Olivia. It seemed Olivia the X was part of Dash's past too.

"Is that right? How do you know Olivia?"

Dash nearly pitched face forward onto the front lawn when I said her name. Apparently he thought *old friend* would be the end of the conversation.

I'd never seen anyone search so hard for some kind of explanation. I almost felt bad for him. Mom managed to step in and erase any discomfort with a brisk topic switch. "I'm going to be baking at Elsie's this evening. You should stop by later at Lacey's house for some coffee and petit fours." Mom was practically twittering with enthusiasm for her plan. "Wouldn't that be nice, Lacey?"

"I'm sure Dash has more important things to do than sample petit fours." I sensed immediately that I'd hurt Mom's feelings and wanted to step back a few seconds in time. "I mean," I said, quickly, "I know Dash would love to taste your baked creations, Mom. They are wonderful but Dash is busy. In between work hours, he's remodeling his house. Besides, there are old friends to catch up with." I couldn't resist the final jab.

Dash looked as if he would have given anything to take back his decision to walk over and talk to us. I decided to help him out of his predicament.

I patted Captain on his head. "You should get going. I'm sure Captain is anxious to go on his walk."

"Yes, I'll let you two ladies go too. Have a good rest of the day." Dash's green eyes flicked back my direction as he turned to leave. I couldn't read his expression but it was rare to see Dash uncomfortable or not at ease. For the longest time, I told myself to stay out of the fray between Dash and Briggs. I enjoyed both of their friendships but Olivia's arrival had sparked my curiosity. There was more to the story with him and Olivia the X. I was determined to find out the beginning, middle and end.

CHAPTER 26

*A*fter dropping my very giddy Mom off at Elsie's, I discovered Dad next door at Coffee Hutch.

Dad and Les were sitting on one of Les's tall pub tables sipping coffees and looking windswept and sunburned. Les was wearing one of his signature Hawaiian shirts, one that was mostly bright red. I could barely see the difference between the red fabric and his face.

"Lacey," Dad piped up when he spotted me. "You just missed that detective fella. He was asking about ya." I knew Dad was tired when he was saying words like fella and ya. He might have been exhausted, but it seemed he was having a great time with Lester.

"He was asking about me? Interesting." It was possible Briggs had something new on the case. It was a perfectly legitimate reason to go down to the station to see him. I first sat with Dad and Lester.

"Sure is horrible to hear about Jenny Ripley," Les said. "She was an awfully nice person. Always came in every Wednesday for some hot tea and lemon."

I nodded. "She struck me right away as someone who was just permanently kind. That's why this is an especially baffling case. How was it today? Lots of fish biting?"

They snuck secret grins toward each other as if they'd been friends forever. I knew they'd get along well, and I was so pleased to see it.

"Not much success at the end of the fishing line," Les said. "But we had a great time."

I reached over and pressed my finger against Dad's cheek. It turned white and then red again. "And, I see it was such a good time you forgot about sun block. You do realize Mom is going to have a conniption fit about this sunburn."

Dad shrugged. "Yeah but it was worth it. I'm going to head home and shower. I'm invited to a game of poker tonight with Les and a few of his friends." Dad leaned closer and whispered for dramatic effect. "But I'll leave the poker part out when I mention it to your mom."

"Don't think she'll hear anything you say, Dad, because she'll be blinded and rendered speechless by that lobster face you're wearing."

Les laughed. "Elsie's going to give me an earful too. She takes such good care of her health and her skin."

I climbed off the bench. "Well, they are baking petite fours right now, so you boys have a few hours to try out some foundation or come up with some good excuses for not using sun block."

"I've got one," Dad said. "I hate the way that stuff smells. Makes my eyes water. If my eyes were watery, I wouldn't be able to catch fish."

Les elbowed him. "Which you didn't catch regardless." They both broke out in laughter.

I waved and walked away.

"Where ya going, kiddo?" Dad called.

"I'm going to see why that detective fella was looking for me."

Les muttered something to my dad that was obviously not meant for my ears. I was sure the topic was Briggs and me. I ignored it and headed toward the police station.

Briggs' car was out front, signaling he was in the office. I walked inside. Hilda, the woman who ran dispatch and the front desk peered up over the chin height counter.

"Lacey, haven't seen you in awhile. I was just asking Detective Briggs where you'd been and here you are. Nice to see you."

"Nice to see you too, Hilda. Do you think he has time to see me?" I was suddenly and unexpectedly nervous about seeing him.

"Let me check." Hilda got up and knocked on the office door. She went in and popped out seconds later. I half expected her to say he didn't have time, but she buzzed me through the gate and waved me past.

Detective Briggs was sitting behind his desk. It was obvious there was still awkward tension between us when he popped up to formally welcome me into his office. Not that he didn't usually stand but there was something far more stiff about his greeting this time. I decided the easiest way to put to rest the awkwardness was by getting straight to murder business.

"Thought I should let you know that I have definitive proof that Molly was cheating in the pie contest." I reached his desk. He motioned for me to have a seat in the chair across from him. "By definitive, I mean I tasted the pie sample she entered and the pie baked by Mayfield Bakery. They were the same pie."

He jotted the information down in his notebook, but I got the sense that he was doing it to be polite so as not to brush off my information as useless.

"I know it seems like a silly motive, but I'm certain that's what I saw Jenny and Molly arguing about the night Jenny was shot. Molly might have worried about being shamed by the town when they found out she cheated. Maybe she shot Jenny to save herself the embarrassment." I shrugged. "Just a theory."

"A theory that gets dissolved quickly by the fact that Molly has an alibi. She was working in the salt water taffy booth at the time of Jenny's murder."

I sank down some. "Oh, yeah, that."

"Yep. It's a good alibi."

"And Carla was with her husband at the time. And there are neighbors to verify that so I can skip my theory about a crime of passion motivation. Vernon did have the picnic with Jenny just the night before. Even knowing it upset Carla."

"Yes, I'd say she has a solid alibi too." He flipped through his notebook. "If private citizens could have a page for Yelp reviews, Jenny would have all five star ratings. People were genuinely fond of her. It's hard to find a motive when everyone adored the victim."

"Makes it even more tragic then, doesn't it? She was a good person. I know I liked her instantly." I sat forward and rubbed my chin. "Wait, aren't we forgetting—there is one person who had a bone to pick with Jenny."

Briggs flipped to a page in his notebook. "Percy Troy, her neighbor. I was just about to head out to Jenny's house and talk to him. Would you like to come along?"

I practically choked on a gasp of air. I covered my mouth to stifle a cough.

"Or maybe you don't have time," Briggs suggested.

"No. I mean yes, I do have time if you don't mind me tagging along." The overly polite and conciliatory conversation was ridiculous. We'd always had such an easy time talking to each other. I hated that things had gotten rough and unnatural between us.

"I don't mind at all. I'm going to have a look around Jenny's house as well." He grabbed his shoulder holster off the hook by the door and his coat off the chair and got ready to go out. "How were the fireworks?" he asked.

It seemed an odd topic for him to mention since he'd stood me up for our date. Maybe he was just trying to make conversation.

"Other than it ending with murder, it was very nice. Loud but exciting. My parents and I had a nice time."

"That's great. And, Lacey, I am sorry about that night. I had every intention of watching the show with you."

"Briggs, let's just solve Jenny's murder and leave other stuff behind for now."

He paused at the door and looked at me. It was hard to stay angry at him when he used those brown eyes to apologize. But I wasn't quite ready to be un-mad.

"You're right. Let's go solve this thing, Miss Pinkerton."

CHAPTER 27

*T*he car ride to Jenny's house was polite and formal and nothing like our usual time together. Our pets became the easy, safe topic of choice and because his dog, Bear, was a large, silly pup and my crow was extraordinarily human-like it helped fill some of the drive time with light humor.

Briggs looked over at me. "You're certain?" he asked. "Kingston has a crush on the Fruit Loops bird?"

"I can't think of any other explanation for him staring longingly at the box. He doesn't care for the cereal at all. And the toucan is a fairly impressive bird, as far as birds go."

Briggs chuckled as he parked in front of Jenny's house. It seemed my crow and his obsession with a cereal logo had helped lighten the mood between us.

We climbed out of the car. With the heat of summer drumming down on her untended, un-watered garden, the flowers were starting to wilt. "Her friend Carla let me know that Jenny kept a key under the front mat." He shook his head in dismay. "Because no thief would ever guess that."

"Spoken like a true man of the law. But just for the record, there is no spare key under my welcome mat. Mostly because I'm not organized enough to have a spare key."

"I was just about to congratulate you, but I guess I'll hold my accolades."

Briggs and I walked up to the house. He noticed the half removed stone wall and the few posts for a new fence. There was no one working on it.

"I rode by here in the morning," I said. "Mostly for a little exercise. I noticed that Percy was no longer working on the fence. I'm sure he decided it wasn't necessary if his neighbor was no longer around to make sure it happened."

"He was building it himself?" Briggs asked before stooping down to lift the mat. He pulled out the key.

"Yes, Jenny told me he was very cheap. When the judge ordered him to pay for the construction of the new fence on the real property line, which falls three feet on his side, Percy decided to build it himself. I guess there was no time limit put on construction because it seems to be going at a snail's pace. It looks exactly the same as it did when I came here for the garden club meeting. I met Percy that day too, by the way."

"Yes, I know Percy. He's been into the station occasionally to complain about this and that. Usually just trivial things like the trash men leaving the cans too far in the street and barking dogs. He's what one might call a curmudgeon. That's why I'm surprised he's building that long fence himself. I can't really picture him out there swinging a sledge hammer or pouring cement."

Briggs unlocked the door. The house was stifling hot and the smell of bacon scented the room. "This has been my first chance to get to Jenny's house. We've been trying to track down her sister. She lives in Australia. She's the only next of kin."

Briggs left the front door ajar to allow some fresh air to flow through. We split off. I was still thinking about the pie so I went to the refrigerator. Sure enough, the remainder of the bakery pie was sitting inside the fridge on one of Jenny's pretty porcelain plates. Even when she was trying to expose a cheater, she did it with quaint, sweet style.

"Are you looking for something in particular?" Briggs asked from the front room. He was going through her address book. "Or are you just hungry?"

I shut the refrigerator. "Funny detective man. I'm still thinking about the pie contest. The Mayfield Bakery pie is sitting in her refrigerator. She had all the evidence she needed to accuse Molly of cheating."

"My detective instinct says the pie scandal is a dead end." He flipped through the pages of the address book. "One thing you can always count on with the older generation is they keep their contacts in an address book. Jenny knew a lot of people."

"Uh huh, and my amateur detective instinct tells me the phone book is a dead end. Unless you're going to call each person and get an alibi."

"Funny amateur detective woman." He snapped the book shut. We'd somehow worked past the awkwardness brought on by the lost kiss and Olivia the X showing up. But there was still plenty to discuss about that night. For now, it was better left behind.

"What did the coroner and forensics say?" I asked. "Anything of note?"

"The bullet was old. Possibly ammo from World War II. If we had the gun that would really help."

I snapped my fingers. "Did you say World War II?"

"Yes. Do you know someone who has antique pistols?"

"I sure do. Jenny." I led him to the room. All of her cute pillows were piled on the daybed. It was a sad sight, like her lonely kids waiting for her to come home. "Her father left her a World War II artifact collection." It felt slightly disrespectful going through her prized possessions but then I reminded myself it was all to find her killer.

I opened the closet. The polished walnut box with the commemorative pistol was front and center. "Jenny gave us a little tour of her collection on Monday after the garden club meeting." I pulled forward the box and lifted the lid. Her father's collector edition Colt 1911 was missing along with four of the bullets.

I turned to Briggs. "It was here when she showed us the collection. Do you think the poor woman was shot with her father's prized possession?"

"We don't know that for sure but I'd say it's highly possible. Who else was here the day she showed you her collection."

I thought back quickly. It was only three days earlier but so much had happened since then, I had to picture the scene inside the room. "Well, there was me." I looked pointedly at him. "And Molly, the pie cheater. Carla was here. She seemed more interested in the embroidered pillows than the war memorabilia." Another name popped into my head. I inadvertently slapped Briggs' shoulder in my excitement. "Oops. I just remembered, Percy Troy showed up just as Jenny was showing us the collection. He saw the gun too. I have to say he didn't seem as angry as I would have expected considering he'd lost a court battle with Jenny. He was polite and genuinely interested in seeing the collection."

"What happened next? After she showed you the collection?"

"I needed to get back to work. The others were still looking at the stuff when I left. But Jenny walked me to the door to see me out."

"So everyone else was left alone in this room?"

"Well, not alone. They were all in here together." My shoulders dropped. "Sorry I can't tell you who left last. Darn it. That would have saved us a lot of time and trouble."

"You can't blame yourself. It's not like you could've predicted that someone would steal Jenny's gun and later kill her with that same stolen gun. You might very well have given us our list of possible suspects though. I'll come back with gloves and an evidence bag for the box." We walked down the hallway. "One thing is for certain, I want to talk to Percy Troy."

CHAPTER 28

*B*riggs gathered the empty box from Jenny's collection and put it in the trunk of his car. I stayed on Jenny's property as Briggs went to talk to Percy Troy. I didn't have any good reason for tagging along and decided not to intrude. In addition, Percy saw me the day of the garden club. He knew I'd been standing in the back room looking at the collection too.

I decided to turn on the hose and water some of the desperate looking flowers in the front yard. I held the hose over the soil beneath the sweet peas. I was still stunned that the gun had been stolen right out from under Jenny's nose. Who would be sinister and cold enough to steal Jenny's inherited gun and eventually kill her with it? It showed a good deal of premeditation on the part of the murderer. Was it symbolic? Did the person hope Jenny would see the gun before it fired so that the last thing she saw was the barrel of her dad's prized commemorative Colt? Only that wouldn't have happened because the cowardly killer shot Jenny in the back. Maybe it was good that she hadn't faced down her nemesis, if for no other reason, she didn't have to die knowing it was her dad's gun and bullet. Molly had a harsh personality but even she didn't seem to be that cruel.

A loud knock brought my attention over to Percy's porch. It seemed he wasn't at home. Or maybe he was hiding in a back room avoiding a direct conversation with Detective Briggs.

"Hello?" a voice yelled from out in the field.

It was neither. Percy Troy was standing at the end of the long stone wall. He had a sledge hammer leaned against his shoulder. His cap and shirt were stained with sweat. He took off his work gloves and walked toward the houses.

"Briggs," I called to the front porch. "Percy is out there working on the wall."

I turned off the hose and followed Briggs out to meet Percy as he hiked in with his sledge hammer. He wiped his forehead with the back of his forearm and blotted his neck with a bandana he pulled from his pocket. He reached us and took off his thick glasses. A piece of cloth was tucked into his shirt pocket. He proceeded to wipe the lenses.

"Were you looking for me, Detective Briggs?" Percy asked.

"Yes, Mr. Troy. If you have a minute, I need to ask you some questions. It's about the death of your neighbor, Jenny Ripley."

"I figured as much. I'm surprised you only just got out here."

"Yes, well we we've been working on notifying next of kin."

"Jenny doesn't have many of those." Percy put his glasses back on. They made his eyes look giant, like the one's Carla wore. "Terrible tragedy. Still can't believe it." He added a tongue click for good measure.

"Mr. Troy, did you attend the fireworks show down at the marina on the fourth?"

A dry laugh shot from his mouth. He stopped it quickly, apparently deciding it wasn't appropriate in this setting. "Excuse me for that. I never go. It's too loud. Too crowded. Besides, I can see the whole thing just fine from my front porch and I don't even have to look for parking."

Briggs wrote something down. Percy stretched his neck up to try and see what was written. "So you were here the whole night?"

"Yep. About half past eight, I made myself some popcorn and came out here to watch the show."

"Was anyone else here?"

"Nope, just me and my parakeet, Timber. He stayed inside. He doesn't like loud noises. I had to cover his cage before the explosions started."

Briggs looked around. The houses were far apart. The neighbor he was closest to was Jenny. She had obviously not been at home.

"Mr. Troy, can you think of anyone at all who might have seen you here on your porch between eight and nine?"

Percy wiped his forehead again as he scrunched it into deep lines. "No. Why? I'm not a suspect am I? I know we fought about that darn wall, but Jenny's been a pleasant, good neighbor. She used to bring me cookies. I always rolled her garbage out to the road. Even did it this week."

"You're not a suspect," Briggs said calmly. "But we are trying to narrow down a list of people who might have had a motive and the opportunity to kill Jenny Ripley."

"Well, I hope you catch them. I'd sure like to know how a woman could get shot in the middle of a crowded holiday festival. Maybe you boys down at the station need to be more vigilant." Briggs had stepped on a nerve, and Percy was on defense. Just like Molly and Carla had become instantly defensive about his line of questioning.

"Yes, thank you for the advice, Mr. Troy."

I could always count on a cool as a cucumber response from Detective Briggs.

Briggs tapped his notebook with his pen. "By the way, Mr. Troy. Did you see Jenny's collection of World War II artifacts?"

Percy's giant bug eyes rolled my direction. "Yes. She was there too." he pointed rudely at me. "And Molly from down the street and that other woman, the tall one."

"Carla," I supplied the name for him.

"Yes, that's the name. I'd come over to ask Jenny about the fencing material I was choosing. She mentioned that she was showing her friends the collection. I told her I was interested in antique guns so she invited me in to have a look. That Colt 1911 is a beauty." His eyes seemed to shift upward with an idea. "I wonder if they'll be having an estate sale with all her things. I'd sure love to get my hands on that Colt."

Briggs cleared his throat. "Hardly the time to talk about that, Mr. Troy."

Percy looked properly chastised. He dropped his face and kicked lightly at some dirt. "Of course. You're right."

A car turned the corner onto Maplewood Road. I recognized it as Molly's. She turned into her driveway. Briggs still had a few questions for Percy, so I decided to stroll down a few houses and chat with Molly. My intuition told me she had something to do with the case. I wasn't sure why I felt it. I just did.

CHAPTER 29

$\mathcal{M}$olly looked less than pleased to see me as she stepped out of her car. She immediately glanced past me toward Jenny's house and blanched when she saw Detective Briggs' car out front.

"What's going on, Lacey? Are they arresting Percy?"

I reached her and instantly noted that she smelled like vanilla. She also seemed agitated, like a kid caught with her hand in the cookie jar. Her cheeks were flushed as if she'd just run around the block.

"No arrest. Detective Briggs is just talking to him." Molly was in the room when Jenny displayed her dad's Colt. She was still there with Percy and Carla when Jenny walked me out. I tried to read her expression, but her shifty eyes and occasional nervous lick of the lips made it impossible. She wasn't acting herself. And Briggs was so quick to end my theory about the pie contest motive.

"Why? Do you think Percy had something to do with Jenny's murder?" I asked. I knew the answer, of course. She was quick to

146

toss his name out as a suspect when Briggs questioned her the night of the murder.

Air blew from her lips. "Who else could it be? I can't tell you how often he complained to me about having to put up that new fence and how his property was losing value in the process. They fought over that fence for a year before Jenny took him to court. I can tell you things got pretty nasty between them for awhile."

"Really? Percy mentioned that other than the fence issue, Jenny and he were good neighbors. He rolled her garbage can out for her just this week."

"That's only because Jenny kept her can right near his bedroom window. In the summer, he could smell it through his screen. He took it out early so he wouldn't have to smell it."

"So Jenny didn't bring him cookies on occasion?"

"I'm sure she did. You know Jenny, she made a big batch of her oatmeal raisin cookies every month. She always gave a plate to everyone on the street." Molly reached into her car for her purse. As she straightened, I caught another whiff of vanilla or something pretending to be vanilla. "That's why I can't believe someone would kill her. Just doesn't make sense."

She pushed her hair away and hung the purse on her shoulder. As her hair swept back, I noticed a pink mark on her neck. My high school years were behind me, but I could still recognize a hickey when I saw one. Molly quickly pulled her hair down over her neck to cover it. I knew very little about Molly's personal life except that she was no longer married and she had two kids in college. It seemed now I knew more than I wanted to know.

"Did they get a hold of Jenny's sister?" Molly asked.

"I think so."

"I wonder what will happen with her house. I hope they don't sell it to some developer. This is a nice, quiet street." Molly was just as callous as Percy talking about the house like he talked about the gun. Jenny had sure deserved better neighbors. I would have mentioned something about it being too early to talk about the sale of Jenny's house, but something told me Molly wouldn't feel the least bit contrite about it.

"Molly, remember when we were looking at Jenny's World War II collection?"

She shifted on her feet, reminding me of Kingston when he had done something naughty. "Yes. Why do you ask?"

It wasn't my place to mention the stolen gun, but I tried to work around that to see if she remembered the details of that afternoon.

"Jenny walked me out. Percy, Carla and you stayed behind in the room."

Molly glanced toward her house. "Is that my phone?"

"I didn't hear anything."

"I should get inside. I've got laundry to fold."

"Just real quick—do you happen to know who was last to leave that room?"

My questions were starting to irritate her. "I don't know, Lacey. I can't remember something so trivial. It might have been Percy. I certainly had no interest in that stuff," she said in a huff. "And frankly, I don't care to be questioned out here on my front yard by someone who has no authority to question me at all."

Angry and harsh from Molly I was used to but cagey, defensive and nervous? I'd never seen her like this. "You're right, of course, Molly. By the way, did you have fun baking today?" I took a whiff. "Sugar cookies?"

Molly looked utterly baffled by my question. "I don't know what you're talking about. I rarely bake, and I certainly wasn't making sugar cookies on a hot July day."

I grinned at her for a second to see if she caught her own misstep. She was too flustered by the entire conversation.

She'd given me my in. "Interesting how someone who rarely bakes is always ready to enter a pie in the pie contest."

"Clearly, I meant cookies. What are you implying anyhow?"

"Jenny found out that you were using the Mayfield Bakery apple pie for your entry."

Her nostrils flared. I wondered if I'd stepped too far.

"It's hardly a motive to kill someone," she snapped. "It was just a stupid pie contest. No reward except a blue ribbon. Maybe you should talk to the person who loses the contest every year. Carla enters every year, and she loses every year. Maybe she was mad at Jenny for always picking my pie."

"You mean the Mayfield Bakery pie?"

I'd stepped on the final nerve.

"As I said before, I have chores to do." Molly held her purse against her. A hint of vanilla wafted along with her as she sidled past me.

I headed across to Jenny's front yard. Briggs was standing alone under the shade of the porch writing down a few notes. He looked up as I approached. His hair looked slightly wild in the breeze traveling up from the shore. Wild was a good look on him.

I met him in the porch shade. The sweet peas were giving off their candy scent in appreciation for being watered. "Find anything of interest to write down in that cute little notepad of yours?"

His lip turned up on one side at my choice of adjectives in regards to his official notebook. "I've got a few details in my cute little notebook. From what Percy remembered, they all left the back room with the closet where the gun was stored about the same time. He said there was a short conversation between Jenny and Carla about having Jenny make Halloween pillows for Carla, but they left the room together. He can't remember who closed the box or the closet door. He thought it might have been Jenny." He looked up. "That was Molly Brookhauser you were talking to, right?"

"Yes, the pie contest cheat. She is sort of an unpleasant woman, but she was acting particularly defensive and snippy today."

"Maybe she felt as if she was being interrogated," Briggs suggested.

I placed a hand against my chest. "Me? I would never be so obvious. She was doing a lot of shuffling and lip licking like she was hiding something. Without letting her know the gun had been stolen, I asked if she remembered who left the room last after we looked at the collection. She thought it might have been Percy, but she didn't put a lot of effort into remembering details of that day. I suppose I might have made her feel as if she was being, you know, like you said."

"Interrogated?"

"I don't know if I'd use that word. Interrogation always conjures images of harsh lights and stern looking cops ready to brow beat you to blurting the answer they're looking for. Let's just say she felt 'put upon.'"

Briggs chuckled and shook his head. "Put upon," he repeated quietly for another laugh. We headed toward the car.

"I confronted her about the pie cheating contest," I said.

"No wonder she felt 'put upon.'" He opened the passenger door for me and walked around to the driver's side.

"She provided me with the ideal segue," I continued as he sat in the driver's seat. "I asked her if she'd been baking because she had this odd scent of vanilla on her clothes. She snootily answered that she rarely baked."

Briggs started the car. "The pie contest winner doesn't bake. Guess that was a good slip of the tongue."

"It was. So I thought, why not bring up the store bought pie."

He tilted his head side to side. "Makes sense. Still the pie motive is thin, at best. Now I need to see if the bullets in that box match the one Blankenship found in Jenny. That way we'll know for certain the murderer used her father's Colt."

CHAPTER 30

The afternoon visit to Jenny's house had proved fruitful. It had also lightened some of the tension between Briggs and me. It almost felt as if the whole thing was behind us. Even though I knew it wasn't. The last thing I expected after feeling at ease all afternoon was for Briggs to bring it up.

"Lacey, I need to talk to you about the other night. After the picnic," he said to clarify, though it wasn't really necessary.

I'd been brushing off his attempts and avoiding it like a silly kid. It was time to drop the stalling tactics. I looked over at him. He was staring straight ahead as he drove along Culpepper Road back to town.

"Since my only escape is jumping from a moving car, I suppose I can listen this time."

He reached up and tugged lightly at his collar to loosen it. "As Olivia mentioned, we were married for a brief time."

"Brief time?" I asked.

"Just over a year. We were a couple in high school."

"Let me guess—football quarterback and head cheerleader?"

He cleared his throat. "Something like that. I'd convinced myself it was true love and meant to be and all that foolish stuff you can believe when you're eighteen. I proposed right after graduation. We married quickly after that. Not sure what the rush was except I was heading off to the police academy and I just thought I needed to be married. Maybe to show I could handle being a grown up. Not sure what I was thinking."

"Lots of people get married to their high school sweetheart."

He turned the corner at the town square, but instead of heading to the station he parked under some trees and opened the windows so we could talk. "That's just it. The more I think about it, Olivia wasn't really my sweetheart. She was popular and extremely beautiful."

I shrugged. "I don't know if I'd use the qualifier *extremely* but she is beautiful."

He smiled. "Yes, I learned the hard way the more you know about her, the less beautiful she is. Besides, it's the woman's character and personality that count most."

I turned slightly to the side and gave him a raised brow. "Said no man ever in the history of men. And I think if I deeply analyze that statement, I might be somewhat offended."

His brown eyes widened. "What? No. Wow, I'm making a mess of this." He did something I wasn't expecting, and it knocked the wind from me. He took hold of my hand. "Lacey, when I see you, my whole day lights up no matter the weather. You have to know that."

I could feel a warm blush start at my neck and work its way to the top of my head. "I'm always happy to see you too, James. Even if most of the time there is a dead body between us."

He smiled as he released my hand. I could still feel the warmth of it on my palm. "Not the best of circumstances for cultivating a relationship."

I blinked at him. "Is that what this is then?"

His throat moved with a nervous swallow. It was nice to see that the question was so important to him he was thrown off his usual cool, calm balance beam. "That's what I'm hoping for. What about you?"

I rolled my chin back and forth to let him know I was thinking about it. Though I really wasn't. I'd been hoping to finally break through the friendship only barrier for some time. It seemed we were finally at that point. "Yes, it's what I want, but I need to know, James. What happened between you and Olivia? Was it just your youth and jumping into something straight out of high school?" I was digging. Maybe it wasn't my place to do so, but it seemed important to understand.

Whatever the truth was, it must have been a doozy because he shifted in his seat and stared out through the windshield at nothing in particular. I was just about to give up thinking I would learn about his marriage breakup when he took a deep breath and turned to me.

"This will clear up more than one mystery," he said. "Dash and I were not just acquaintances in high school. We were best friends."

"I gathered that."

Briggs looked surprised. "Really?"

"You can't have a deep seated dislike for someone, unless, at some point in time, you had a strong affection for the person. And believe me—deep seated doesn't even touch the surface. I can't even bring up his name without red flames shooting out of your ears."

"My ears do not shoot flames. Although, as a kid I used to wish that I could shoot them from my nose like a dragon. And I'm sorry for acting like such a numbskull. I think seeing Olivia again has made me realize, I need to let the anger go."

I looked out toward the marina where Dash worked. I couldn't see him on any boats but then it was early evening. He was probably at home hiding, trying to avoid my mom. I turned back to Briggs.

"So the end of the marriage had something to do with Dash?" He didn't need to respond. The latent hurt and betrayal was in his eyes. "Guess I don't need too much imagination to connect those dots," I said. "I'm sorry, James." My opinion of Dash had just taken a sharp turn south. "I thought better of Dash. It seems I've been mistaken."

"No, Lacey. That's not why I told you. I don't want this to ruin your friendship with Dash. This is not all on him. And a lot of time has passed. I never thought I'd have to talk about it or bring it up to you, then Olivia showed up out of the blue."

I turned more to look at him. I contemplated telling him that I saw Dash and Olivia having coffee but quickly put an end to the idea. "And exactly why did Olivia show up?"

"Her uncle's funeral. She lives on the east coast now with her husband. A lawyer in a big firm. Definitely more suited to her than a high school quarterback heading to the police academy."

Was there hurt or regret in his tone? I couldn't tell. He was always so blasted calm about everything. At least now I knew she hadn't come back to rekindle an old flame.

I laughed. "This is totally embarrassing to admit, but I actually allowed myself to consider that I was the source of your animosity toward each other. I think Lola and Elsie kept putting that in my head. I let this head grow big and bloated enough to occasionally believe it." I turned forward. "There you go, humiliating confession time over."

Briggs was staring at the side of my face. I stared straight ahead, not wanting to make eye contact quite yet.

"I've got news for you, Miss Pinkerton, you were a big source of our renewed anger. Dash and I have hardly seen or spoken to each other for years. I never even gave him much thought anymore, and I know he never gave me a second thought either. Then Lacey

Pinkerton showed up to town and old wounds reopened. But I promise to do better."

I turned to him. "You're not just making this up because of your extremely beautiful ex-wife?"

"Would I lie?"

"I guess not since you're a detective and all. I should get back. Mom is at Elsie's bakery. They are making petite fours together."

"Petty what's?"

"Petit fours. Cute little cakes." I held up my fingers to show the approximate size of a petit four."

He squinted at the space between my fingers. "It should be a crime to make a cake that small. They are getting along, then? Elsie and your mom?"

"Gosh, I hope so. I'm counting on Elsie to be the more mature of the two."

"Yes, the same woman who told everyone they could come eat treats with Mr. Darcy on Valentine's Day."

I laughed. "Oh my gosh, I forgot all about the Mr. Darcy calamity. But it worked out in the end."

Briggs started the car. I was feeling a hundred percent better about Briggs but a hundred percent worse about Dash. Of course, a good detective always listened to both sides of the story. One day, I'd ask Dash about what happened back then. It would be interesting to hear the story from his side. But I still was never going to feel the same about my charming, handsome neighbor.

CHAPTER 31

*W*ell, it was happening and it was my fault. Now that Lola and Ryder were officially a couple, my best friend was spending a whole bunch of time in the flower shop just lingering and making sparkly eyes at her new boyfriend. I wasn't too annoyed, yet. I had a bigger worry. I knew Lola, she tended to jump in with both feet and search for the life preserver later. Lola had a major crush on Ryder right from the start. When he returned the interest, she backed away, scurrying off in fear. Now the opposite was happening, and I worried things were moving too fast for both of them. But I was going to keep positive thoughts and hope for the best.

Lola's giggles twittered down the short hallway to my office. Lola was not normally the giggle type but for Ryder she managed a good long set. I finished up my purchase orders. It was a slow week because of the holiday landing right in the center of it, so I had a few minutes to make a graphic for the murder case. Sometimes it helped me to look at all the pieces and connect the parts.

Jenny's missing gun was a major development. If it was indeed the murder weapon. That still needed to be clarified, but for my graphic, I made it the killer's gun. The garden party was on Monday. That was the day Jenny showed the four of us her prized collection. Since Jenny was shot on Wednesday, chances were the gun was stolen the day of the club meeting. That narrowed down the list of suspects considerably. I could cross my name off because I knew I wasn't the killer. That left Molly, Carla and Percy.

"Knock, knock." Lola popped her head into the office. She was now both a giggler and a person who said 'knock, knock' instead of actually knocking. "Are you busy?"

"Actually you caught me doing something that has nothing to do with the flower shop."

"Uh oh. I won't tell the boss though." She was practically skipping as she entered. (Skipping—also not a normal Lola thing.) She dropped heavy into the chair across from my desk. "Just thought I'd say hello before I went back across the street."

I looked up and waited.

"Hello," she said. Then she leaned forward. "Oh my gosh, he is such a doll," she whispered. "So funny too. I can't stop laughing when I'm with him."

"So I noticed."

"Wait, am I laughing too much? Shoot, I don't want to seem silly. Should I tone it down?"

"No, be yourself. It's fine. Just don't move too fast."

The chair scraped the floor as she scooted it closer to my desk, as close as her knees would allow her to get. "Are we moving too fast? I'm going to blow it. I always do. I just know I'm going to ruin this."

I glanced toward the door. The shop bell rang. Ryder started talking to the customer. I still lowered my voice considerably. "Lola, just be yourself. Don't over think this and for goodness sakes, relax. Ryder is an easy going guy. So are you when you're not in the throes of hysteria. Like right now. Deep breath and stay natural. If it works out great and if doesn't, it's not the end of the world."

I should have stopped at the word great. She sat forward so fast her knees smacked the desk. "Do you think it's not going to work out?"

"I didn't say that. Stop second guessing yourself. You're awesome. He's awesome. It a great match."

Lola finally relaxed some. "You're right. I've got to let things happen naturally." She sounded resolute but I wasn't counting on her to follow up on that. "New subject. Did you try the petit fours? Elsie brought me a plate this morning, and I've been buzzing on a sugar high ever since. She said she had a wonderful time with Peggy Pinkerton."

"Yes, my mom didn't stop talking about Elsie all morning. And yes, I was dropping those petit fours like M&Ms. One bite cakes are brilliant. As long as there are a lot of them on the plate. My mom said she was going to spend the morning online shopping for athletic shoes and sportswear so she could start running. She wants to be fit and trim and full of energy like Elsie. But between you and me, my mom runs circles around me. If she has any more energy, we're going to have to get her one of those hamster wheels in human size. Anyhow, she's started new exercise regimens many times. They usually end quickly with a pulled muscle because she dives into everything so enthusiastically, she ends up getting hurt."

Lola laughed. "Gee, where have I heard that before?" She pointed up to her chin. "Oh yeah, right here. But now that we've talked, I'm determined to cool my heels some. Take things slower. Starting now. I need to head back to the shop and leave Ryder to his work." She stood up. "Oh hey, did you ever find out why Detective Briggs' ex-wife was in town?"

I decided not to tell the whole story of the marriage breakup. It wasn't really my story to tell. "I guess she's in town for an uncle's funeral. She lives on the east coast. So we won't be seeing her much after this."

"The flower shop owner said with a sigh of relief," Lola quipped.

I had to nod in agreement. I waved my fingers at her. "Go run your shop before Late Bloomer hires a new store manager."

"I wish. Then I could just be some squirrely helper who gets to dust the antiques and answer the phone instead of holding the weight of the world on my shoulders."

"Oh? Business not going well?"

"I just need to put my parents in a different mindset. Less centuries old, garish, ornate stuff and more modern, simple furniture and lamps. But that is my cross to bear not yours. You have a murder mystery to solve." She motioned to my paper with the graphic and names. "My money is on Molly. She's always a grump. Later."

"Bye." I stared down at my paper. I'd written Jenny's name in a circle in the center and the three possible suspects in boxes around the circle. All three of them had access to the gun. Motives for everyone were weak at best. Carla was upset at Jenny because her husband always bid on Jenny's picnic basket. Otherwise, it seemed Jenny went out of her way to be a kind and supportive friend to Carla. Percy had a much stronger motive than the other two. He had lost a court battle over a dividing wall, and he had to give up some of his property as a result. That meant money and money was always a good motive for murder. (If there was such thing as a *good* motive for murder.) Percy was also the only one of the three with no real alibi. He was at home with his parakeet but no one saw him. Molly had just a slightly stronger motive than Carla and the picnic basket problem. Jenny had caught her cheating in the pie contest. And even though there was little reward, other than the honor of being the best pie baker for the contest, it would have been humiliating for Molly if the town found out. Of course, there was the one of a kind hat debacle where both Molly and Jenny agreed not to wear the rhinestone hat to the festivities, then neither stuck to their promise. Again, hardly a reason to kill someone. And the hard truth of it all was that both Molly and Carla had solid alibis for their whereabouts during the fireworks show.

I sat back and tapped my pencil against my chin trying to come up with anything else pertinent, but I was drawing blanks left and right. I folded the paper but could still see my writing through the back. Molly's name lined up over Jenny's. Seeing the two names over each other sparked a far out idea. It was about as crazy and far-fetched a notion as I'd ever had. Jenny and Molly were about the same height and weight. They were both wearing the same hat on the night of the murder. Jenny was shot from behind. What if the killer was after Molly and accidentally shot Jenny? While Molly was less agreeable than Jenny, why on earth would someone want to kill her?

That question brought me right back to the start.

CHAPTER 32

The morning passed quickly. Before I knew it, Mom and Dad showed up for the lunch we'd planned. As we strolled to Franki's Diner, Mom told me all about the running gear she bought for her latest foray into the world of fitness, and Dad worked hard not to comment on how much money she'd spent on her last exercise ventures.

Franki spotted us the second we walked in and marched right over with hands on hips and signature beehive tilting slightly to the right. "Well, Lacey Pinkerton, I wondered when you were going to introduce me to your parents." Her stern expression fell away. She went straight for a hug from each of them before I had a chance to introduce anyone.

Franki stepped back. "In case you missed the nametag, I'm Franki."

"Franki, my parents, Peggy and Stanley."

Dad glanced around at the vintage decor. The whole restaurant was an explosion of red vinyl, polished chrome and white laminate. "I love this place already, and I haven't even tasted the food." Dad smiled at Franki. "Which I've heard is fantastic."

Franki blushed. "Why, thank you. Here, let me show you to a table, and we can get you set up with one of our delicious lunches." Franki led us down the aisle of seats. She looked back at Dad. "I think you'll like our chili and cornbread. All made from scratch."

Mom leaned over and whispered in my ear. "He'll love it but after a few hours, I'll be sorry about it."

I elbowed her and laughed. I pointed out the red diamond tile pattern running beneath the counter. "Hey, Mom, does that remind you of anything?"

It took her a second. "Yes, that looks just like our first kitchen. It's adorable in the diner but not so great in a house."

"Ah, I loved that red diamond pattern."

Franki led us to a booth near the end of the room. She placed down the menus as we slid onto the seats, Dad and I together and Mom across, facing the direction of the entrance.

"I just brewed some raspberry tea," Franki said.

I picked up the menu. "Sounds good."

"Yes, please," Mom said. The second Franki walked away something else caught Mom's eye. She gave me a little kick under the table. "There's your neighbor. Should we invite him to sit with us?"

"No," I said so abruptly even Dad looked up from his menu. "No," I said quietly.

"Hello, Dash," Mom said cheerily. I tapped her foot hard under the table. She scowled back at me.

Dash stopped at the last seat on the counter, just across from our table. He turned to us.

"Hey, Pinkertons, nice to see you again." His green eyes landed directly on me. "Lacey," he nodded.

I returned a nod but it was so slight it could easily be missed.

"How are the boats today?" Mom asked. "That's what you do,

right? Fix boats?" Sometimes I loved my mom and sometimes I wanted to pretend I didn't know her.

"Yes. And the boats are good. Thanks for asking."

"That's nice," Mom said. "Oh and if you're interested in some petit fours, there is a tray of them in Lacey's refrigerator. In fact, maybe Lacey can bring some by later." She blinked big eyes at me. I didn't respond and lifted up my menu.

"Have a great lunch," Dash said.

My shoulders relaxed with a sigh when Dash turned back to his stool. As we waited for our three orders of chili and cornbread, I got a text. Mom tried to give me the 'not at the table' scowl but those days had long past. I picked up the phone and read the message. It was from Briggs.

"I've got some news on the case. Can you get away from the shop for a bit?"

I texted back. "I'm eating lunch at Franki's with Ma and Pa Pinkerton. I can walk over right after. I've got another wacky theory."

"Looking forward."

"Can I bring you something from Franki's?"

"No, I ate a sandwich at home. Bear is just starting to recover from the fireworks noise. I should have named him Lion. Cowardly Lion."

I sent back the smiley emoji. "See you soon."

I tried to have an enjoyable, fun lunch with my parents, but I was hyperaware of the man sitting just a few feet away. Mom kept looking at him, then she'd sweep her eyes toward me and then back to Dash again like she was watching a tennis match. I was sure she was hoping if she looked back and forth enough she could create a line of romantic sparks between us. She was persistent, if nothing else.

When Dash decided to take his lunch with him, I was finally able to relax enough to enjoy the chili. That was after Mom created a scene with her good-bye and vocally lamenting that Dash wasn't staying to eat his lunch. Can't imagine what made him decide to take it to go.

Dad had finished his cornbread, and he was not-so-secretly eyeing mine. Franki came to the rescue with another plate of it. "I was in the kitchen and I looked through the window and saw your bread plate was empty but you still had chili. You must be a corn-bread dunker, and you can't eat chili properly without something to dunk."

Dad's grin was a mile wide. "Lacey, I might just have to move to this town."

Franki looked pointedly at me. "See, you should have brought them in earlier. I kept thinking—when is Lacey bringing her parents into the diner? I was starting to feel a little neglected to be honest."

"I'll make it up to you by bringing them in for lunch tomorrow," I said.

"Perfect." Franki looked at Dad. "I'll bet you like a good cheese-burger. And I make my own ketchup."

"Oh yeah," Dad said, "I've been known to like a good cheeseburger."

Normally, Mom would have chimed in on Dad having an almost flirty conversation with another woman, but she was too busy watching Dash head back to the marina with his bag of food. She was completely oblivious to the conversation at the table. I hadn't planned on telling her, or anyone, what Briggs had told me. But I thought it might tamp down her matchmaker enthusiasm if she knew.

Franki walked away and Mom started in about Dash. "I think you hurt your neighbor's feelings. It was clear he wanted to sit at the table with us."

I shook my head. "That was only clear to you. I didn't see it at

164

all. I'll tell you a few things, Mom, and you can't say one word to Elsie or anyone else. Not even Kingston or Nevermore."

Mom wiggled in her seat and picked indignantly at her corn-bread. "Why on earth would I be saying anything to your pets?"

"Just this morning you told Nevermore that he was eating too fast and that he'd get hiccoughs." Dad took a bite of the new cornbread.

Mom flared her nostrils gently at him and returned to me. "You can tell me. I'll try not to blab it around town since you seem to think I am some kind of loose-lipped-loon."

Dad laughed and then shoved another piece of cornbread into his mouth to stifle it.

"I hardly think you're a loose-lipped-loon. Boy, try and say that ten times fast, eh?" I looked sparkly eyed at Mom, but her mouth was in a straight line. She wasn't going along with my attempt at humor.

"Dash is very charming and good looking and he has come to my rescue more than once. I enjoy talking to him."

Mom's smile grew with each compliment. For some reason she seemed to think my list was leading to an 'and that's why I'm nuts about him' instead of a 'but there's something you should know'. Her smile vanished when I ended with the latter.

"I know you had a bad first impression of Detective Briggs because, well, you broke, through the police line," I added and then wished I hadn't even mentioned it.

"There was no line." She was sticking to that *line* of defense.

"Yes, anyhow. Dash and Detective Briggs, James—" I clarified. Using his official name was probably not helping her warm up to the man. "They were good friends in high school. Played football together. James married his high school sweetheart right after graduation before he went to the police academy."

Mom sat back. "Uh huh, so he's married anyhow?"

"No, not anymore. They divorced quickly."

"Fresh out of high school marriages rarely last," Dad added a rare nugget of opinion before concentrating on his chili.

I sipped some tea. "I'm sure youth had something to do with it." I looked plainly at Mom. "But Dash had something to do with it too."

Dad caught my meaning instantly but Mom was perplexed. She was still wearing star covered glasses when it came to Dash.

I lowered my voice. "I don't have any details and I don't want them either, but apparently, Dash and James' wife Olivia were seeing each other on the side."

Mom was still not letting the bad stuff through. She wasn't quite ready to give up on my neighbor. "What side?"

Dad dropped his cornbread in the chili and grumbled about it before looking up at Mom. "For pete's sake, Peggy, what side do you think? They were having an extramarital affair." He said it just loud enough to gather some attention from nearby tables. Fortunately, no names were mentioned, otherwise I'd probably just have to pack up my shop and house and move on.

Mom looked positively deflated as she processed the news. Then she scooted forward and straightened her shoulders. "I knew that Dash was no good the second I laid eyes on him."

Dad and I just stared at her with open mouths. There wasn't any point in arguing or reminding her that she was practically writing out our wedding invitations only an hour earlier.

Franki came to the table with the bill. "I gave a twenty percent discount for my special guests."

"Oh, you didn't need to do that," Mom said.

Dad kicked her shoe under the table and picked up the bill. "Thank you so much. It was delicious."

Franki grinned from ear to ear. "Wonderful. Is there anything else? More tea?"

Mom lifted her glass. "Yes, please, it's so refreshing."

"Not me, Franki, thanks. Mom, Dad, I need to hop across the

street to the police station to ask Detective Briggs something before heading back to work."

Mom placed her hand on my arm. "But we just sat down."

"Gosh, I hope not," Dad said as he looked at the array of empty dishes in front of him.

I kissed her cheek. "I have a shop to run, remember? Thanks for lunch, Dad. I'll see you guys at home."

I waved to Franki and headed outside. My phone buzzed as I crossed Franki's parking lot. I was surprised to see it was a text from Dash. "Any chance we can talk?"

"About what?"

"I just want to tell my side of things."

"Fine."

"I'm off at seven. Can you come to the marina?"

I knew he was picking a location far from home because a certain someone would never let us talk in peace. "Yes, I'll be there."

"Thanks."

I stared at the phone a second. I had no idea what he could possibly say to make his side of the coin shiny, but I had to at least give him a chance.

CHAPTER 33

*H*ilda was taking down the red, white and blue streamers hanging along the front counter. She made an attempt to spruce up the drab, pedestrian front desk at every holiday. I thought it was cute.

I grabbed a fluttery end of the streamer and helped her roll it up. "I think Detective Briggs is expecting you."

"Great."

Hilda had the gate to the office propped open with her chair. I handed her the roll of streamer and walked through to Briggs' office. During the short journey across the street to the station, I'd gone back and forth mentally several times about whether or not to tell Briggs about my meeting with Dash. I never came to a solid decision.

I knocked on the door.

"Come in," Briggs called.

He stood up with a smile. It felt like things were back to the way they were before Olivia showed up. "How was lunch with the parents?"

I nearly leapt into the embarrassing narrative about lunch with Mom and Dash in the same diner but then reminded myself Briggs probably wouldn't find it amusing or entertaining. "It was great. I think my Dad is secretly planning to ditch my mom and run off with Franki and her chili and cornbread."

"Franki does hold a magic spell over most of us with that chili, cornbread combo. You said your mom is a great cook. I'm sure she has a few magic spells of her own."

"Not with chili and cornbread. Although I'd bet any amount of money that when she gets home she'll make chili and cornbread just to show him he was making a big deal about nothing." I sat in the chair. "You said you had some news on the case."

"Yes I do." He opened a file folder on his desk, pulled out a picture and spun it around. It was a gun inside an evidence bag. Even though I'd only seen it for a few moments in a velvet lined box, I could tell it was Jenny's Colt.

"That's the commemorative gun from Jenny's collection. How? Where?"

"Ivan Perez, the old guy who combs the beach every week with his metal detector was running the device close to shore. It beeped like crazy and he followed it. The gun was mostly buried in the sand right where the water breaks."

I pushed the picture back to him. "That's it then. You have the murder weapon. Jenny's inherited antique Colt."

"Yes. We don't know for certain if the person who stole the gun was standing in the room that day, but I went back to the house this morning and checked for signs of forced entry. I didn't find anything. The thief would have had to know exactly where Jenny stored the gun."

I tapped the arm of the chair with my fingers. "If it was one of the three people in the room, then Percy had to be the killer because Molly and Carla have alibis."

"That's where my mind was going. He also had a stronger

motive than the two women. Only I didn't get a strong sense that Percy was angry at Jenny. Even with the fence issue. We've got the weapon, but I still have a weak case. Not sure why this one feels so disjointed."

I bit my lip as I tried to decide whether or not to mention my latest theory. He knew me too well.

"You've got something on your mind, Miss Pinkerton." When we first started working together he insisted on calling me Miss Pinkerton. He kept up the habit whenever I was assisting him on a case. I'd grown to like it. Especially when he used it in a sort of fun way, like now.

"Well, Detective Briggs, I've got an outlandish idea. Only, the more I mull it over, the less outlandish it seems. It also doesn't help solve the murder."

"Go ahead," he prodded. "I'll take anything at this point."

"To explain this right I have to start back at those matching hats. You know Jenny's patriotic, rhinestone bedazzled cap?"

"Yes, it's in the evidence room. Nate said she fell and hit her head after the gunshot. That's why she had a mark on her forehead, and her hat was damaged too."

"Like I told you, she bought the hat from Kate Yardley. Kate told her it was one of a kind and then proceeded to sell one almost exactly like it to Molly. Molly showed up at the garden club meeting with the hat. Jenny was quite distraught that she was going to be wearing the same hat to the festival. Particularly because Kate told her it was unique."

Briggs nodded. "Sounds like Kate."

"Jenny confronted Kate about it but Kate fluffed it off. She said there were differences in the rhinestones and size of the stars or something like that, so technically, they were one of a kind." I rolled my eyes to let him know how I felt about Kate's sales technique.

Briggs leaned back on his chair. "You don't think Kate had anything to do with Jenny's murder?"

"What? No. Not at all. Kate does her own thing. She's not exactly friendly, but she didn't kill Jenny. Anyhow, Jenny and Molly decided they couldn't possibly both wear the hat to the festival."

It was his turn to roll eyes.

"I know. I thought it was silly too, but they made a promise to each other to not wear the hat on the fourth. Naturally, they both showed up wearing the hats."

"Of course. So you think Molly was mad that Jenny wore the hat? That's almost weaker than the pie scandal motive."

"I agree. But that's not my theory." I sat forward. "What if the wrong person was killed? What if the bullet was meant for Molly and not Jenny?"

Briggs rubbed his chin between his thumb and forefinger as he contemplated my suggestion. "They are about the same size and if they were both wearing the same hat . . ."

"Jenny was shot in the back so the killer might have thought it was Molly."

I startled when he slapped his desk. "And Molly was supposed to be in the booth at that time but she never showed up."

I nearly jumped from my chair. "Wow, I forgot that detail. That makes my theory even stronger." I reached back and patted myself on the shoulder.

"Good job on that, Pinkerton." He stared down at the file on his desk. "But that makes it even harder to find the killer because we don't know for sure that the wrong person was shot. Why would someone want to shoot Molly?"

"Hmm, good question. Although, she is far less likable than Jenny." I snapped my fingers. "Molly was terrible to Carla at the garden club meeting. She humiliated her in front of all of us because Carla had planted dahlias in her garden. The dahlias were already blooming and Molly said garden club members should always plant from scratch."

Briggs' forehead rose. "So no one can wear the same hat and no planting flowers in the garden unless they come from seeds. Are you certain this is a good club for you?"

"It's not a club at all without Jenny. All I know is that Molly went out of her way to be rude and mean to Carla. Jenny came to Carla's rescue, but I could see there was no love between Molly and Carla."

"There's a slim motive there but we're back to Carla having an alibi. She was with her husband and neighbors during the fireworks show. The garden club booth was in a remote location. It had been a special request from Jenny. She preferred the booth be under a tree and away from the press of the crowd. But even so, it would be impossible for someone to shoot a gun and not be heard unless there was a loud noise like fireworks to mute it."

"Those alibis sure do get in the way of solving cases, don't they? So it's back to the original—Jenny the victim. Percy the killer."

"It seems so."

"I should get back to the shop. Thanks for filling me in on the gun discovery."

"And thank you for the wrong victim theory. It was a good one."

I stood up. "Even though it didn't lead us anywhere."

"You never know." He got up to walk me to the door. My earlier mind debate about Dash came back to me. I decided not letting Briggs know was almost like lying to him.

"James." I always knocked him off balance by saying his name. This time was no different. I might have done it to let him know something big was coming. Or maybe it was because the topic wasn't anything to do the investigation. Or maybe I just liked the way it sounded. For whatever reason, I had his full attention so there was no turning back. "Dash texted me. He must've realized that I know about Olivia. The truth is I saw them having coffee together in Mayfield." I waited for some kind of reaction but didn't get one. I was absurdly glad that he didn't seem to care that they'd met for coffee. "Anyhow, he wants a chance to tell his side of the story." *There* was the reaction I'd been looking for. A hint of anger in those otherwise calm brown eyes. "I told him I'd listen. I just wanted you to know."

Briggs nodded once. "Thanks for telling me." He was trying hard to stay true to his promise to not always react negatively to my friendship with Dash. That friendship was on such a thin, fragile thread, it was more of an acquaintance at the moment. "I'll see you later. What will you do next in the investigation?"

"Jenny's sister is in town. I'm meeting her at Jenny's house and hoping she can shed some light on the case. Not holding out for too much though. She's been living in Australia these past ten years. They only saw each other once a year."

"Yes, that doesn't sound too promising. But I'm glad Jenny has someone here now. It's such a lonely thing to die without family around."

"I agree." He walked me out to the front office. I turned to smile at him and thought right back to that kiss I never got. Darn Olivia the X and her bad timing.

CHAPTER 34

*A*fter a long day at work and a quick dinner at home with my parents, I pulled my bicycle out for a ride to the marina to see Dash. With the long summer hours, I'd have plenty of time to get back home before dark. I didn't plan on staying long. There just couldn't be that much for him to say. I didn't dare tell Mom that I was meeting him. She was angry enough with Dash that she hadn't even mentioned him once at dinner.

I pedaled down Harbor Lane. It felt refreshing to ride in the cool of the evening. Most of the shops were closed and there was sparse traffic. Lola and Ryder had gone to dinner so her shop was dark and locked up like mine. Briggs' car was still parked in front of the station. He was working late again. I hadn't told him I was meeting Dash at the marina. The less details the better. I sensed he wasn't exactly thrilled about my talk with Dash but he seemed to understand why I'd agreed to it.

I hadn't left my house until seven, figuring I'd make Dash wait a bit. He was sitting on the bench across from the bicycle rentals looking a little lonely. He was rarely sad, but I saw it in his face as I pushed my bike along the pier. As I passed the ice cream shop, the door opened and Carla's husband, Vernon, almost raced out. He glanced around quickly sending the intense smell of his sun block through the air. I said hello but he walked past with his head down as if he hadn't seen me. Or as if he didn't want me to see him. Maybe Carla didn't like him eating ice cream. He was a nervous man, that was for sure.

"Sunset is going to be nice tonight," Dash said as I walked up.

I glanced out toward the water. A thin layer of clouds had painted the sky gray and pink like watercolors. I leaned my bike against the railing and sat next to him.

"Thanks for coming."

"I'm always one to listen to both sides of a story," I said. "Just not sure what you can say to flip this your direction."

He sat forward and rested his arms on his thighs, then leaned back. "Actually, can we walk? I'm feeling kind of fidgety."

"I noticed." I stood to let him know I was game for a stroll. Right then, the heavy, sweet smell of ice cream filled the air as the door swung open. This time Molly walked out. She looked around too but was far less agitated than Vernon.

"Hello, Molly," I called across the pier.

Her eyes swung around to find the voice. "Oh, hello, Lacey." She took a moment to shine a smile at Dash and then hurried off.

"Must be a good night for ice cream," I said, but Dash's mind was elsewhere.

We walked toward the marina where most of the boats had already docked for the night. Out at sea, a gray smudge of smoke had marred the colorful sunset. Burt Bower and his painfully loud fishing boat were rolling into shore. Like clockwork, just as Briggs had said.

The noise pulled our attention out to sea for a second. "It's a wonder he can catch any fish at all," I said. "If I were a fish, I'd be terrified if I heard that monstrous boat."

Dash smiled. His usual easy laugh seemed to be hiding this evening. "I'm sure Briggs told you about Olivia and me."

"He mentioned it." I added just enough chill to my tone to let him know how disappointed I was in him.

"I have no defense for it. Briggs and I were friends in high school. Good friends. I looked up to him. He was a great quarterback, a great student, an all around popular guy. I envied everything about him. He was just smooth and easy going no matter what. I think, deep down, I wasn't just envious but jealous. I could never be him."

"Oh come on, Dash. Are you kidding? Every head turns when you walk down the street. You've got the charm to go with the looks. How could you possibly have been jealous?"

"Because Briggs just had that whole cool thing going that I could never figure out how to replicate. And he had Olivia. I'd had a crush on her for a couple of years, but she only had eyes for Briggs. He got so busy in the police academy he didn't have much time for her and she started calling. We hung out together. I still had a crush on her. I should have just said no. But I didn't. I was only nineteen. All those feelings, envy, jealousy, crushes disappeared once I realized I was my own person and that I didn't need to strive to be anyone else. Guess it just took me a long time to mature."

"Only a man truly comfortable in his own skin would admit to that, Dash. I understand that this all happened when you guys were young and—" I paused because my voice was drowned out by the thunderous clatter of Burt Bower's boat.

Dash motioned for me to follow him farther away from the noise. People on the pier and in the marina were shooting Bower angry glares, but he just moseyed into the slip, taking his time to get the boat in just right.

Dash and I walked along and reached the grassy knoll near the tree where the garden club booth had sat when Jenny was shot.

The clamor from Bower's boat still made it hard to hear each other but we talked loudly.

"Like I said, I can forgive the teenage Dash. It's not me you hurt. It's Briggs. He's the one who needs to hear this." Bower finally turned off the engine. The tension in my shoulders fell along with the noise. "Isn't there anything you can do to fix his boat?" I asked.

"Yes but he's too cheap to hire me. He keeps fixing it himself. And you're right about that. I should talk to Briggs, offer an apology of sorts, but things are still too strained between us. The arrival of the very appealing town florist didn't help that much either."

It took me a moment to realize he was talking about me. "What do I have to do with that?" My attention was caught by a man, another boat owner, shouting at Bower on the pier. It seemed people had every right to complain. It was so loud it drowned out every noise within a mile radius.

"Oh my gosh, Bower's boat." In my excitement, I grabbed Dash's arm. I released it quickly.

Dash looked back at the marina. "It's turned off now. The smoke always hangs around until the breeze carries it off."

"No, that's not what I meant. Dash, if I fired a gun right here while Bower was pulling into the marina, do you think anyone could hear it?"

He laughed. "I think you could shoot a canon from this hillside and no one would hear it over that boat."

"Exactly." I clapped quickly. "I think you just helped me with a major revelation about the murder case."

"Great. At least I scored on that. About what I was saying earlier, Lacey."

"It's all right, Dash. We can still be friends. I've just got a slightly different view of you than I had before. But everyone makes mistakes." I smiled up at him. "Sometimes even really big mistakes." I hated to cut off our conversation. I knew somewhere in there he had thrown in something about the new girl in town, namely me, but I had a murder to solve.

"I can see you're ready to take off. I've got the truck if you want to throw your bike into the back, I can give you a ride home." We headed back to the pier where I'd parked my bicycle.

"Actually, I need to stop by the station and talk to—"

"Briggs," he filled in for me. "You don't have to be so secretive or hesitant about it. I know who the better man was this time—again. Now that I'm wizened and mature, I accept defeat much more readily. I take some comfort in knowing your mom thought I was the better match. She might have mentioned it in passing. Actually not in passing. She told me straight out."

"Ugh, my mom. And, by the way, about that—" This time my hesitation was not going away. He seemed genuinely pleased to have garnered my mom's approval, and I hated to burst that bubble. He deciphered my pause on his own.

"So she knows too?"

I half smiled.

"Great. Think I'll go hibernate in my house until the stink of my past wears off."

"Mom doesn't hold grudges long. One of your captivating smiles and a warm hello will probably do the trick. She's sort of a pushover for handsome, charming men. Guess most of us are." I reached my bike. "I'm glad we talked, Dash. Living right next to each other, I think it's important to stay friends."

"I agree, Lacey. Thanks for letting me talk. Be careful on the way home. It's getting dark."

"I will. See you later."

CHAPTER 35

I rounded the corner and was relieved to see that Briggs was still in the office. Hilda and Officer Chinmoor had gone home for the night, so I texted him to let him know I was out front.

He walked out of his office. I was happy to see him not just because of my brilliant new theory but . . . just because I was happy to see him.

"Lacey." He looked past me and saw my bike leaning against the light pole. "It's getting dark. You rode your bicycle down to the beach at night?" He stepped out of the way to let me pass.

"It's not night. It's evening." I hadn't told him any of the details of my meeting with Dash. I didn't see any need to elaborate. I had more important things to discuss. On the short bike ride to the station another light bulb went on that had to do with Vernon, Molly and Vernon's vanilla scented sun block.

We walked into his office and I sat down. "What brings you here tonight? A new theory?"

"Yes and not just a new theory but a brilliant new theory. In fact two brilliant new theories." I held up two fingers for a visual.

His half grin was back again. I'd sure missed it. "Go ahead, I'm all ears."

I realized as I started that I was going to have to give the details of my trip to the marina. I decided to just rip off the bandage and tell him. "Remember when I told you Dash wanted to talk to me?"

"Like it was scratched in my brain," he said with less of a half grin.

"Right. Well, that's graphically put but good to know you remember." I took a deep breath. "He asked me to meet him at the marina. Mostly, I think, to avoid my mom's intrusion into our conversation. She sort of latched onto Dash once she met him."

He picked up a pen and made it into a teeter totter on his thumb, signaling he wasn't loving this whole conversation.

"Anyhow, none of that is important. Halfway through our conversation, Burt Bower rolled in on his calamity of a fishing boat. As you well know, it's so loud, it's impossible to hear anything over it."

The best thing about the way Briggs and I worked together was that our minds almost always came to the same conclusion at the same time. I'd only given the introduction to my theory, and I could already see the thrill in his eyes.

He dropped the pen and sat forward. "The murder didn't happen during the fireworks."

I crossed my arms and tilted my head. "I came up with it first. The least you could do is let me blurt that out."

"Sorry. Pretend I didn't say it." He sat back. "You were saying, Miss Pinkerton?"

"What if the murder didn't take place during the show?" I bit my lip. "See, the whole ta-da moment is gone. Lucky for you, I have one more big, giant nugget of brilliance, and there's no way for you to get there first because you weren't on the pier just now."

"What happened on the pier? And if at all possible, leave you-know-who out of the story."

I blew out an audible breath and rolled my eyes. "Glad you're working on that forgiveness thing. Anyhow, Vernon Stapleton walked out of the ice cream shop. He looked around suspiciously. He was wearing that strong smelling sun block that he coats his skin with. I could smell it because it has the distinctive smell of vanilla. Moments later, after Vernon had left the pier, Molly Brookhauser came out of the ice cream shop. She didn't look quite as guilty but that doesn't matter. Yesterday, when I talked to Molly on her driveway, she smelled like vanilla. Only, not baking vanilla. Vernon's vanilla scented sun block. Molly once bragged that she never wore sun block but she certainly had on some of Vernon's. Accidentally, it seems."

Briggs' brow lifted. "So Molly and Vernon are having an affair?"

"It seems highly likely. She had a red mark on her neck yesterday that she was working hard to hide behind her hair."

He laughed and then opened his notebook. "Then the alibis from the two women are useless if the murder happened before the show. Considering how Bower always pulls in at 7:30 we have a much smaller window for the murder. It takes him about ten to fifteen minutes to get that shambling noise machine moored.

"What if our first hunch was right and Molly was supposed to be the victim instead of Jenny?" I asked.

"Then we'd have a possible motive if Vernon's wife knows about the affair. But we don't have proof of that either. I need to ask both Molly and Carla where they were in the hour before the fireworks show. Once I know that, it'll be easier to connect things." He got up from his desk and picked his coat up off the chair.

"Where are you going?" I asked.

"Thought I'd head over to Molly Brookhauser's house and see if she has a new alibi." He stopped and looked at me. "Are you coming? After all, this started from your new brilliant theory."

I hopped up. "Woo hoo. Can I put my bicycle in the office?"

"I'll put it in my trunk. It'll be too dark for you to ride home after this."

We managed to get the bicycle into the trunk and more importantly we got the trunk to snap shut after three good tries. I slid into the passenger seat wondering what Molly would do when she saw me drive up with Detective Briggs. She wasn't too happy with me showing up to her driveway yesterday. But then Molly was rarely happy about anything. Except maybe ice cream with Vernon.

I knew the subject of Dash would come up on the way to Molly's. And it did.

"So you and Dash talked?" he said casually as if it hardly mattered.

"Yes and he is remorseful and embarrassed and trying to blame his youth. Which he does have a point there because we all do stupid things when we're young. And old. Let's face it—stupid is in human DNA. He did confess that he always looked up to you. In his own way, he wanted to be just like his friend James Briggs."

Briggs shook his head. "I don't know why. Dash was popular. He could sweet talk his way out of any detention slip. The women in the cafeteria piled extra mashed potatoes and gravy on his plate. Even the school secretary rarely marked him tardy because she liked him so much."

"I just know what he told me."

Briggs looked my direction. "And you believe him?"

I turned to him. "I have no reason not to. He's never lied to me."

"I suppose you're right. By the way, Olivia is back home now so you won't see her strolling through town anymore."

I watched his profile to see if I could read how he felt about that. There was nothing.

"Do you miss her?" I asked.

"No. We've hardly spoken in years, and I'm fine with that."

Briggs turned the car down Maplewood Road. Molly's porch light was on but the house was dark. Her front door was open.

Briggs parked the car. "Why don't you stay here while I see what's going on." He climbed out and walked toward the house. He stopped on the porch and knocked on the open door.

Molly's scream broke the quiet. Briggs drew his gun out of the holster and raced inside. I climbed out but stayed near the car. My heart was thumping wildly. Worry urged me forward. I crouched low and moved toward the front of the house. Loud footsteps pounded the floor in the entryway. I ducked down next to the steps and held my breath as Carla stumbled out the front door swinging a hammer around like a madwoman. She found her balance and ran down the steps. I stuck my foot out at the bottom and sent her flying face first onto the lawn. She landed with a thud just as Briggs burst out of the house after her.

Before she could get up, he had her hands behind her back. "Carla Stapleton, I'm arresting you for attempted assault."

Molly came to the door, whimpering and sobbing and looking white as a ghost. I hurried up the steps to lend her support.

"I don't understand it. Why would Carla try and kill me?"

I turned toward her. "I think you know."

The grim white pallor was quickly replaced by an embarrassed blush.

Briggs called for a female officer for backup and helped Carla to her feet. Her face was beat red as she zeroed in on Molly. "It was supposed to be you. Not Jenny."

It seemed Molly might collapse from shock. I braced her elbow with my hand.

Carla continued with her rant that was turning into a confession for murder. "That stupid hat tricked me. You and Vernon have been carrying on long enough, making a fool of me." Carla's bad eyesight and the matching hats had caused a terrible tragedy.

Briggs walked her to his car reciting her rights as he led her away.

I walked Molly back into the house and into her kitchen. She sat down while I got her a glass of water.

She looked dazed. "I don't understand. So I was supposed to die and not Jenny?"

"Seems that one of a kind hat saved your life but cost Jenny hers."

Molly turned pale again. I gave her the glass of water, which she readily drank. Red lights and sirens lit up the quiet country road. It seemed Detective Briggs and his assistant, Miss Pinkerton, had solved another murder case.

CHAPTER 36

I hugged Mom and Dad and then Mom once more for good measure. They climbed into the convertible. "Remember to come for Thanksgiving," Mom reminded me for the hundredth time.

"I won't forget."

Briggs' car pulled up just as we were saying our final goodbyes.

Mom tugged my arm. "There is that detective again." She leaned to look at him in the side view mirror. "Looks like he has a box of chocolates. But flowers are more romantic."

Dad rolled his eyes. "Hey, Peg, did you happen to notice that your daughter owns a flower shop?"

"Oh right," Mom said. "In that case, chocolate is very nice."

Briggs reached the car. "Mrs. Pinkerton, I just wanted to apologize for the other night." He handed her the box of chocolates. (I admit, I was a tad disappointed.)

Mom made her usual scene, hand to chest and all. "Oh my, you didn't need to do that. I was intruding on your work. You had every right. But thank you so much. Really wasn't necessary."

Dad stepped in to stop her from gushing. "Sorry, we didn't get to talk more Detective Briggs. My daughter speaks highly of you." He pointed his Dad finger. "You make sure she stays safe and out of trouble."

Briggs smiled. "I will do my best. Though the trouble part might not be easy."

Dad got a kick out of that. "Don't I know it." He started the car. "Take care, kiddo."

Mom reached for my hand. "Bye, sweetie."

"Call when you guys are safely home." Briggs and I waved and watched as the convertible pulled out of the driveway and turned onto Myrtle Place.

"No chocolate for me, I suppose?"

He pulled out a tiny gold box. "I picked up a few truffles for you."

"Yum." I led him to the porch. "How about a glass of iced tea?"

"Sounds good."

Nevermore was in one of his many daytime hideouts. Kingston looked up from his nap just long enough to see who had entered and then tucked his beak under his wing.

"Should I be insulted by that greeting?" Briggs asked.

"Not at all. He only acts like a big puppy when he sees Lola. I don't get more than a head turn either, and I feed him and put clean newspapers in his cage."

I walked to the kitchen and poured the iced tea.

"He likes Lola?"

"He adores her. Huge crush."

"So Lola and the Fruit Loops toucan?"

I handed him the glass. Our fingers touched as he took the tea.

"I think his toucan crush has ended. I can credit my dad with that. He got such a kick out of it, he kept holding the box up to the cage to see Kingston's reaction. Now I think King is afraid of the toucan. Like he's a stalker or something."

Briggs laughed. "Don't know if you realize this, but you have a crazy life."

"Oh, I'm fully aware." I placed my tea on the counter and Briggs did the same.

Without warning, he took hold of my hand. His fingers were still cold from the tea but they heated up fast. I could have sworn I felt the warmth run all the way up my shoulder to my face.

"Thank you for your help solving the murder. This one had me baffled but you figured the whole thing out." He squeezed my hand and let it go. I was disappointed he released me.

"It was easy to be baffled considering right from the start we had the wrong victim and the wrong time for the murder."

"Yet, you filled in all the holes. And you saved Molly's life in the process. Good move on the porch, by the way. Even though I told you to stay in the car."

I batted my eyelashes dramatically. "Did you?"

He stepped forward. We were face to face. I was slowly losing myself in his brown eyes when he took my hand again.

"Now, where were we before all the chaos of the week started?" he asked.

"Chaos?" My mind drifted back to that lost kiss.

"Wait. I remember." He leaned toward me and pressed his mouth against mine for a kiss. My knees were like jelly.

After a good, long moment, he straightened. His half smile, the one I adored, appeared.

I smiled in return. "I guess it's true what they say. Some things are worth waiting for."

RED WHITE & BLUEBERRY DELIGHT

View recipe online at: londonlovett.com/recipe-box

Red, White & Blueberry
DELIGHT

Ingredients:

Base layer:

1 pack of graham crackers
6 Tbsp melted butter

Filling:
8 oz cream cheese, softened

1 container cool whip (8 oz)
1 cup powdered sugar
1 tsp vanilla
2 cups sliced strawberries
1 can of blueberry pie filling

Directions:

1. Preheat over to 350°

2. In a food processor, combine graham crackers and melted butter.

3. Spoon a layer of graham cracker crust into your baking dish and press into the bottom. I used 8-8oz mason jars but you can use a pie or casserole dish.

4. Bake in oven for 10-12 minutes.

5. In a large bowl, mix together cream cheese, powdered sugar and vanilla. Then add in the cool whip--works best if it is room temperature. I mixed the cool whip in for a slightly thicker, gooey texture. For a lighter, creamery texture fold the cool whip in gently.

6. Allow the baked crust to cool completely.

7. Once cool, spoon or pipe in a layer of the cream cheese filling on top of the graham cracker crust.

8. Add a layer of sliced strawberries.

9. Spoon or pipe in another layer of cream cheese filling.

10. Spoon blueberry pie filling on as the top layer.

11. Refrigerate until chilled.

12. Serve and Enjoy!

ABOUT THE AUTHOR

If you enjoyed **Dahlias and Death** please consider leaving a quick review on Amazon or Goodreads. Each and every review, no matter how long is incredibly helpful and greatly appreciated.

London Lovett is the author of both the Port Danby and Firefly Junction Cozy Mystery series. She loves getting caught up in a good mystery and baking delicious, new treats!

Subscribe to London's newsletter to never miss an update.

London loves to hear from readers. Feel free to reach out to her on Facebook , follow on Instagram or send a quick email to londonlovettwrites@gmail.com.

Follow London

www.londonlovett.com

londonlovettwrites@gmail.com

f